EVERYBODY TELLS ME TO BE MYSELF
BUT I DON'T KNOW WHO I AM!

Other Books in the growing Faithgirlz!™ library

NIV Faithgirlz! Backpack Bible
My Faithgirlz! Journal

Nonfiction

Beauty Lab

The Sophie Series

Sophie's World (Book One)
Sophie's Secret (Book Two)
Sophie and the Scoundrels (Book Three)
Sophie's Irish Showdown (Book Four)
Sophie's First Dance? (Book Five)
Sophie's Stormy Summer (Book Six)
Sophie Breaks the Code (Book Seven)
Sophie Tracks a Thief (Book Eight)
Sophie Flakes Out (Book Nine)
Sophie Loves Jimmy (Book Ten)
Sophie Loses the Lead (Book Eleven)
Sophie's Encore (Book Twelve)

Check out www.faithgirlz.com.

faiThGirLz!

EVERYBODY TELLS ME TO BE MYSELF BUT I DON'T KNOW WHO I AM!

by Nancy Rue

zonderkidz

ZONDERVAN.com/
AUTHORTRACKER
follow your favorite authors

The children's group of Zondervan

www.zonderkidz.com

Everybody Tells Me to Be Myself but I Don't Know Who I Am!
Copyright © 2007 by Nancy Rue

Requests for information should be addressed to:
Zonderkidz, Grand Rapids, Michigan 49530

ISBN-10: 0-310-71295-5
ISBN-13: 978-0-310-71295-4

CIP Applied For

Published in association with the literary agency of Alive Communications, Inc., 7680 Goddard Street, Suite 200, Colorado Springs, CO 80920, www.alivecommunications.com

Editor: Barbara Scott
Interior Design: Sherri L. Hoffman
Art Direction and Cover Design: Merit Alderink

Printed in the United States of America

07 08 09 10 11 12 • 10 9 8 7 6 5 4 3 2 1

Contents

Who, ME?

Molly Ann McPherson trailed her fingers over the contents of her brand-new suitcase:

A stack of neatly folded — and very cool — shorts.

Another pile of matching tops, the cutest ever.

A pink zipper bag with her own bottles of everything from shampoo to orange-flavored mouthwash.

And the perfect stationery — shaped like flip-flops — so she could write home every day.

Her summer dream was packed in that suitcase. But suddenly Molly shivered in a blast of cold fear.

"I don't think I want to go to camp, Mom," she said.

Molly's mother looked up at her over the swimsuit from which she was removing the tags. "What?" she said. "All I've heard from you for the last month is how much camp is going to rock."

"But I won't know anybody there," Molly said. "What if everybody thinks I'm a loser? What if I don't make any friends? What if I get left out of everything?"

Molly's mom shook her head. "Don't be silly, Molly," she said. "Just be yourself and you'll be fine."

When her mom left to find the sunscreen, Molly stared miserably at the suitcase full of coolness she'd been so excited about.

Be myself? she thought. *Who's Myself?*

Was she the Molly who was careful to do only what the really popular kids did?

Was she the Molly who always agreed with her friends about every little thing?

Was she the girl who secretly dreamed of being a famous lawyer, or the one who took piano lessons because her mom did when she was a kid, or the one who refused to cry in front of anybody, no matter how sad she was?

Molly slumped on her elbows onto her perfect stacks of camp clothes.

"How am I supposed to be myself," she wailed, "when I don't even know who I am?"

now what?

Poor Molly is having a major case of homesickness, and she hasn't even left her house yet. But there's something else going on too, something that can strike any of us, whether we're thousands of miles from our family or sitting in our own bedroom. It's an attack of the "Who Am I's?" and it can be pretty scary.

The good news is that this book is here to help you

* figure out who you really-deep-down-inside are, and

* be that person no matter who you're with.

It's like a vaccine against future attacks.

Right now we have our Molly, suffering the worst case of the "Who Am I's?" ever. If you were there in the room with Molly and her suitcase, what would you say to her? Would you give her advice? Or would you be absolutely clueless what to say because you feel that same way . . . a lot?

Whatever you want to tell Molly, write it in the space below. There are no right or wrong answers, so be honest. If, as you read the rest of this book, you discover something that makes you change your mind about how to encourage Molly, you'll have a chance to "talk" to her again in the very last chapter.

Dear Molly...

Here's the Deal

How many times have *you* heard grown-ups say, "Just be yourself"? Like that's supposed to prepare you for a situation where you don't know anybody, or you don't know what you're supposed to do, or you have that feeling that you are *not* going to fit in at *all*.

In the first place, what do they mean by "be yourself"? They're talking about a thing called *authenticity*. When you're *authentic*,

- ❋ you're completely honest;
- ❋ you don't pretend to be rich, or way smart about something, or totally into horses (or whatever everybody else is into) when you're not;
- ❋ you don't copy the way other kids dress or talk or laugh if it doesn't feel natural to you;
- ❋ you go after the things you're interested in even if nobody else does; and
- ❋ you make up your own mind when it comes to decisions, according to what you know is right and wrong.

That sounds pretty easy, doesn't it? You just do all that stuff and you're authentic.

Yeah, well, if it were that simple, there wouldn't be this book about it, right? Maybe right this very minute you're thinking of one of these problems:

- ❋ What if I'm so honest I hurt people's feelings?
- ❋ What if I just do my thing and everybody thinks I'm weird?
- ❋ What if I always do what's right, and nobody wants to be with me because I'm too "good"?
- ❋ What if I don't even know what I like, and what I'm interested in, and how I want to dress? What about *that*?

Take a big ol' sigh of relief, because this book is here to help you turn every one of those "What Ifs" into a "What Is." You'll learn how to

- ❀ be honest and encouraging at the same time;
- ❀ know what your own "unique thing" is and go for it without caring if other kids think you're weird;
- ❀ show people that "good" is cool; and
- ❀ discover more and more the special, one-of-a-kind person you are... and love you!

Wait... did we just say you're going to love yourself? Isn't that conceited?

Selfish?

Stuck up?

Let's see what God has to say about that.

GOT GOD?

Even if you've only just started thinking about God on your own, you probably know that God-loving people believe God the Creator thought each one of us up, made us, and put us here for a reason. The Bible, where God talks to us, says that over and over. One of the coolest verses is this one:

[God] has shaped
each person in turn;
now he watches
everything we do.
– PSALM 33:15
(THE MESSAGE)

It's fun to imagine God's magnificent hands making an individual person who is totally different from every other baby girl or boy God has created before. Some like to think of God as a potter, shaping people out of clay. God makes a perfect work of art, breathes life into it, and loves it.

God loves what God has made: palm trees, snow leopards, mosquitoes (yeah, even those pesky little critters), and you. God loves you, so how can you do any less than love you too?

"Woe to him who quarrels with his Maker... Does the clay say to the potter, 'What are you making?'"
—ISAIAH 45:9

It's hard, though, with the world telling you to pick yourself apart all the time. Are your clothes hip? Is your slang up-to-date? Are you friendly enough, funny enough, blonde enough? We'll talk more about that later. For now, just remember that God knows how hard it is, which is why God sent Jesus to make everything totally clear. From all the commandments the people had to remember and follow, Jesus got it down to the two most important ones:

"Love the Lord your God with all your heart and with all your soul and with all your mind." This is the first and greatest commandment. And the second is like it: "Love your neighbor as yourself."
—MATTHEW 22:37-39

Basically, if you don't love yourself, you're not going to be very good at loving other people. Loving you doesn't mean you're conceited. It's a requirement! In fact, Jesus goes on to say that all the other commandments are based on these two. If you can't love God with everything you have—and love yourself and other people the same way—you don't have a chance of obeying "honor your father and your mother" (Exodus 20:12) or "do not envy" or any of the rest of them. That could get to be a mess.

Here's the way it works in *God's* world:

✦ God made you beautifully unique, right down to your fingerprints, your voice print, and your designer ears.
✦ God gave the Unique You talents and interests.
✦ God shows you who you are as you get to know him better and better. That's the only way to know the Unique You.

IT (Important Thing):
Moses asked God what he wanted the Israelites to call him. What God said translates as, "I AM WHO I AM." That's what he wants you to be too—exactly who you are. He loves that. So should you.

God wants you to figure out what you're here for. It's part of who you are, who God truly made you to be. And it's something you continue to learn all your life — as long as you stick with God.

If you hate who you are and try to be something or someone else, you grow more false. You move further from your true, beautiful self.

When you love somebody, you want to bring that person joy, right? You bring God joy when you let your real personality and talents shine, instead of hiding them and copying somebody else. Any time you reject any part of your real self — maybe the fact that you're naturally quiet or a true leader — you're telling God he didn't know what he was doing when he created you. Hel-lo-o!

That Is So Me!

So let's start down the path to the Unique You right now. Since one of the most important signs of an authentic person is honesty, here's a chance to practice that. Be totally truthful with yourself as you take this quiz. There are no right or wrong answers, no passing or failing. Your score tells you how close you are this very minute to the path to the real You. That's a good thing to know as you set out on the Unique You adventure.

After reading each situation, circle the letter of the choice that sounds the most like you. Remember to be ... well, authentic!

If I got to decorate my room any way I wanted, I would

    A.   immediately know exactly how I'd have it.

    B.   look at pictures and at my friends' rooms and come up with my own combination.

    C.   find a picture in a magazine and have mine just like that.

If my mom packed raw veggies in my school lunch, I would

    A.   not eat them because I've tried them and I can't stand them (or I'd gobble them down because I love them).

    B.   eat them only if somebody else at my table would eat some.

    C.   throw them away because it isn't cool to eat veggies when everybody else has pizza and french fries.

If I could give myself a different name, I would

    A.   choose a nickname that fit my personality. How cool would that be?

    B.   try on some different names to see how other people liked them before I decided. I think it would be kinda fun.

    C.   name myself after somebody famous. I might still be a little nervous that somebody would laugh at it, though.

If I had to design a logo (trademark) for myself as a class assignment, I would

    A.   love that assignment!

B. be kind of stressed about it until I saw what other people were doing.
C. ask the teacher if I could do something else instead.

If I were asked what color I would use to describe myself, I would say

A. "Hel-lo-o! My favorite, of course!"
B. "Um ... give me a minute to think ..."
C. "What? How am I supposed to know that? I am so over this quiz."

Remember that this quiz just tells you where you are on the Unique You adventure. It's sort of like walking into a mall and looking at the directory with the big star that says YOU ARE HERE. It makes it so much easier to figure out which way you have to go to get where you want to be.

Count up your As, Bs, and Cs:

_____ As

_____ Bs

_____ Cs

On the map on the next page, put a star (*) on whichever point fits you: mostly As, mostly Bs, or mostly Cs.

If you have more As than other letters, you're already on the road to becoming your authentic self. You know a lot about you, and what you don't know, you're finding out. This book will give you some fun ways to learn more, and it will help you avoid wrong turns and dead ends.

If you have more Bs than other letters, you're searching for a way to be you. Right now you may be looking to other people to find out what's cool, what helps you fit in. Even though you may gather information and then make your own decisions, this book will help you depend less and less on what other people think and more on what *you* know is true about you. You're off to a good start.

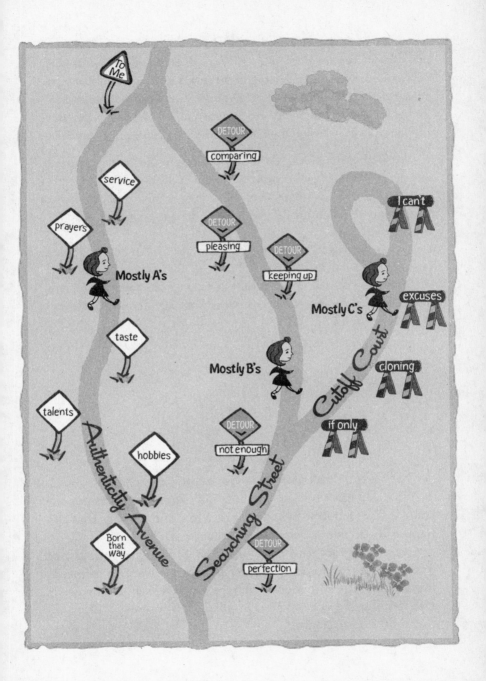

If you have more Cs than other letters, just being yourself might be a little scary for you right now. Don't give up and say you're a born wimp. Take a big ol' breath, say a big ol' prayer, and keep reading. This book will help you shake off the "Who Am I's?" and guide you right to Authenticity Avenue. It's actually a fun journey, and once you're on it, you'll wonder why you were ever afraid.

So, no matter where you're starting on this adventure, you can still get to yourself—your true, God-made self. Even if you're on your way to a dead end on Cutoff Court right now, you can make a U-turn this very minute. All you have to do is keep reading and following directions.

What if you don't? What if it's easier to be who other people tell you to be?

There are several answers to that question. Before we start on our adventure for real, let's find out why it's dangerous to not make the journey at all.

Here's the Deal

If you don't *know* who you are, you can't *be* who you are. And if you can't be who you are, you're going to wind up in some kind of trouble. Below are just a few of the things that can happen if you're not being your authentic self.

You do things you really don't want to do. Most teasing, lying, and gossiping doesn't happen because people just want to be mean. It starts because somebody's unhappy with herself, or she needs attention, or she wants to feel important. If you're just being you, that stuff doesn't matter.

You don't do things you really want to do. You might miss out on some really cool art classes, for instance, if it's more important to you that *other* people won't think they're cool. And that's not all. You might fail to stand up for somebody who's being teased, or fail to stand up *to* someone who's being a bully, because you're not sure if your group will approve. Always checking to see if you still fit can really cheat you out of the places and things and people who are just perfect for you.

You get resentful always having to measure up. Doing your best in school and at home and following the right rules build up your confidence. But if your friends (or the people you want to be friends with) also have requirements for belonging to the group — beyond being yourself — you're bound to start thinking little mean thoughts and snapping at people and generally feeling like you want to smack somebody. And for some reason, the person you say something evil to is seldom the person you're really annoyed with. Yeah, it's a problem.

You never feel quite at ease. There are always nervous questions waving their sweaty hands in your head. "Do I look okay?" "Did I just laugh too loud?" "Do I sound like a geek when I say that?" "If I do this, will they still be my friends?" "I don't know how to act right now!" Pretty soon you're chewing on your fingernails or your hair or your pencils, while the questions keep chewing on *you* from the inside.

As you get older, that anxiety can get more serious. Some girls develop eating disorders, like anorexia or bulimia. Some get depressed. Others always seem to be angry. Still others just load themselves up with activities so they won't have to think about it. None of that makes growing up fun.

Worst of all, if you lose the Unique You that God made you to be, you won't discover what God has planned for you to do with your life. No one who is being her honest, genuine self ever has to worry that she won't figure out what God wants her to do. She'll just naturally do it. But a girl who tries to be somebody else — or a different somebody for every group she's with — may never find out her purpose. That's where the real happiness is, in living out exactly what you were put here for. It would be such a bummer to miss that, wouldn't it?

GOT GOD?

As you go forward on the path to your God-made self, remember this passage, written by John about Christ:

> To all who received him, to those who believed in his name, he gave the right to become children of God.
> — John 1:12

Whoever wants Jesus in her life, believes he is the Son of God, and does as he says; that girl will be her true self, her child-of-God self.

Let's start with that, with knowing God made you to be his child and that's who God wants you to be. Jesus was — and still is — the perfect child of God, and he's the only one we should imitate, just by following his lead. It's the most important thing to know as you set out on your journey.

Ready? Then let's go for it!

An awesome way to see what you already know about yourself deep inside is to make a collage. That's a collection of magazine images you paste together on poster board or paper to create one big picture.

What you'll need:

* a pile of magazines you're allowed to cut pictures from (be SURE to ask permission before you start)
* scissors (or you can tear pictures out)
* paste or glue
* a piece of cardboard, poster board, or paper at least 11" by 14"
* a timer (or just a clock or watch you can see easily)
* a quiet place where you can think and spread things out and not be interrupted (by pesky brothers, nosy sisters, mischievous pets...)

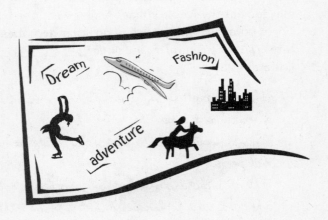

What to do:

* Set your timer for twenty minutes (or look at the clock or watch and jot down what time you start).
* During that twenty minutes, go through the magazines. Each time you come to a picture or some words you really like, cut or tear them out. You don't have to have a reason to choose a picture or words other than, "I just like it!"
* When twenty minutes have passed, put the magazines aside and spread all the pictures and words out on your paper. Rearrange them, sides touching, until they create a picture that pleases your eye. You don't have to be able to explain why you placed the images that way—it just has to make you happy.
* Glue or paste the images to the paper the way you've arranged them.

What this tells you:

* Sit back from your completed collage and gaze at it.
* Rather than looking at each picture and word individually, look at the whole collage as if it were one big picture.
* Try to come up with one sentence that describes the picture. *This is a picture of a person who* _____.
  For example:

  — *This is a picture of a person who is upbeat and cheerful and loves life.*
  — *This is a picture of a person who likes to be quiet and peaceful.*
  — *This is a picture of a person who has a lot of different sides to her personality, from totally wacky to way smart.*

✳ If you need help discovering your sentence, think about

... *the colors.* Are they bright and wild? Soft and pastel? Black and white? What do the colors tell you about your personality that you know to be true?

... *the way you've placed things on the page.* Is it neat and orderly? Scattered and happily confused? Does it make a design? What does your placement tell you about the way you do things that is absolutely right on?

... *the kinds of pictures you chose.* Are they all of one kind of thing? Is there a huge variety? Are they in categories? What does that tell you about your talents and interests and tastes — the ones you may even keep secret from other people?

What to do now:

◎ Put your collage up in a place where you can see it when you're working with this book.

◎ Gaze at it often and see what more it might tell you.

◎ If there is someone in your life who always accepts you for who you are, ask him or her to look at your collage and tell you what he or she sees. Decide if that helps you see yourself even better.

◎ Enjoy your collage. It will help you like the real You more and more.

That's What I'm Talkin' About!

While I was making my collage, I discovered

✦ this new thing about me that I didn't know before: _____

_____

_____

_____

_____

_____

_____

✦ that I'm exactly who I thought I was: _____

_____

_____

_____

_____

_____

_____

_____

_____

chapter two

Mirror,
MIRROR

M olly dragged her suitcase into Galilee Cabin and called
out in a quivery voice, "Hello?"
      No one answered, and that was okay with Molly.
She needed some time to wipe away the tears that started when
her mom and dad drove away and left her here where she didn't
know anybody ...

She sucked in a big breath. What was it Mom had told her?
Whenever she got scared because everyone was a stranger, she
was supposed to say in her own mind: *Just be yourself, Molly.*

Molly hadn't figured out what that was yet, and before she
could get past *I'm Molly Ann McPherson and I'm eleven years old and I
have an eight-year-old goldfish* — the cabin door squeaked open and
three girls pushed and giggled their way in. Like they all knew
each other. Like they all liked each other.

Just be yourself, Molly.

"Hi," Molly blurted out. "Um ... I have an eight-year-old
goldfish."

After they all stared at her for a few seconds, the first girl
said, "That's so cool. I didn't know they could live that long."

The second girl squinted. "They can't. Are you sure you aren't
making that up?"

The third girl snickered and rolled her eyes. She didn't say
anything at all. As far as Molly was concerned, she didn't have to.

Just be yourself, Molly thought as the girls moved on to their bunks, chattering away. *So which one am I? Cool? A liar? Or just a plain old geek?*

That Is SO Me!

As you continue on the Unique You adventure, take a minute to find out what you think of yourself right now. As always, be completely honest. Don't worry about sounding conceited — we already went there, remember? Simply fill in the blanks with the truth.

First, sit or stand in front of a mirror and take a good, long look at the girl staring back at you. Make some faces at her if you want to. Put on your sad expression. Your jazzed one. Your terrified one. Your silliest ones. Show yourself every side of you.

Now . . .

Write down five words that describe the personality of the girl YOU see in the mirror (examples — friendly, quiet, eager, timid, creative):

Think of one thing you like least about your personality and write it down (even if you've included it on the list above):

~~~~~~

Think of one thing you like most about your personality and write it down (even if you've already included it above):

~~~~~~

Write down three things you often hear people say about you (whether they're negative or positive, and whether you think they're true or not):

~~~~~~

~~~~~~

~~~~~~

Ask your mom (or someone else who always accepts you for who you are) to tell you

- two words that describe your personality:

~~~~~~

~~~~~~

- the thing she likes about you most:

~~~~~~

~~~~~~

- the one thing about you she thinks you should work on:

~~~~~~

~~~~~~

continued on next page

continued from previous page

Look over the descriptions you've just written. Think about the following questions. You can write your answers or just chat with yourself about them in your head.

1. What things on your list make you unique? (Even if you think that's the same as strange or weird!) Put a star * next to these.

2. Does your list sound like the You that you know?

3. Were there any surprises, things you hadn't thought of before?

4. Do other people appear to know the real You?

5. Are you different from other people in your family?

6. Are you way different from your friends or the people you want to be friends with?

IT Your image of yourself is going to grow and become more true as you continue your journey. There are some fun surprises ahead of you.

But ... you may also discover a few things about yourself that maybe you aren't so crazy about. That, of course, is because nobody's perfect, and all our lives we have things to work on. Life is one long process of turning up the volume of our best qualities and turning it down on our weak places. Do not put yourself down for being who you are. We're going to help you be the best version of You that you can possibly be.

Here's the Deal

There are tons of ways to get to know yourself so you can be who you are. Want to take a look at some? Here are three major things that form You: (1) Things you were born with, (2) things that come from your family, and (3) the choices you make.

(1) Things That Came in the You Package

Race

If you explore the history of your race or culture, you might be amazed at how it explains pieces of yourself to you. The important thing is that you're headed for confusion if you try to deny your beginnings.

Gender

Being a girl has its own special characteristics. Studies of the brain show that women multitask (do a lot of different things at the same time) better than men, and we can go back and forth from our creative side to our logical side more easily too. You'll love this—girls usually mature faster than boys do (which is why some boys your age seem like absurd little creeps right now).

Age

If you are eight or nine or ten, you probably like facts and learning cool information about science, animals, history—stuff like that. If you're eleven or twelve, you might be thinking about things like feelings, opinions, and why people do what they do. Some of the things you care about now will change as you get older. Your age will always be an important part of knowing yourself and how you're growing.

Some of our unique qualities are inherited. Does anyone ever say that you are just like your father? Maybe you have a quick temper like your mom or the same sense of humor as a great-grandfather you never even met. That doesn't mean you can shrug and say, "Oh, well, that's just the way I am." It's good to be aware of whether these qualities need to be turned down or cranked up. If you're adopted, you may not know. So just claim all your characteristics as totally you, and take responsibility for them.

God gives every one of us a gift. It might not be a rockin' singing voice or a kick-buns pitching arm, but it's something God needs you to use to make the world better or to let people see him. Can you make people laugh without even trying? Are you amazing with little kids? Do you have more energy than any two other girls put together? Can you sense your mom's mood the minute you walk in the door? Finding your gift is the best part of self-discovery.

Why is it that some babies love their first taste of applesauce and others spit it out? Why did you have a favorite color when you were two? Why does one identical twin love rap, while the other is crazy over country music? Because we are all born with certain likes and dislikes. Yeah, some tastes are developed as you grow up (very few three-year-olds dig stuffed mushrooms). But some are just woven into that marvelous creature known as You.

(2) How You're Growing Up

Where you live

Your community shapes you from the moment you're born into it. Living in a crowded city might make you bold and unafraid or careful and suspicious. If you're growing up in a small town, you may not have much fear of other people, or you may be very private because everybody in town knows everybody else's business. The opportunities you have in your little world, the people you know, and your experience with nature give shape to the personality you arrived with.

The way you are raised

You've probably noticed that there are all different kinds of parents. The way your mom and dad's parenting works with your own special personality can be pretty complicated, and you don't have to figure that out. Just know that your mom, dad, and even your brothers and sisters have a huge influence on you.

Your family's personality

Is your family adventurous, always ready for a hike or a new place to go for vacation? Or is it wild and crazy, with hilarious stories at the dinner table and practical jokes happening every day? Maybe yours is quiet and orderly and not very emotional, but totally into something cool like history or animals or science. You might think your family is just "ordinary," but there is no such thing. Check it out.

Religion

How deep your family's faith is has TONS to do with how you use your basic qualities. A faith community full of love and acceptance that guides you instead of just giving you the rules helps you grow into a loving, confident woman of integrity. You can still become that person without the community, but it's easier when you have support. So start praying for that now. God's there for you, no matter what.

(3) The Choices You Make

What you want to do in your free time tells you a lot about your true self. Can you spend hours at your hobbies and be surprised that so much time has gone by? That's a You Thing. Your hobby (or one you'd like to have) tells you that you're sporty, artistic, musical, organized, curious, or just about anything cool you can name. Whenever you do something that gives you joy, you learn something about yourself.

 Hobbies

What do your after-school choices tell you about you? Sports might say you're athletic, competitive, or a team player. The arts could be telling you you're creative or emotional. Clubs may whisper that you're a leader, a joiner, or that you like to serve. Even choosing no organized activities at all could be saying you're independent, a thinker, or a free spirit. Not liking something can speak volumes about you too.

Activities

The people you're with Who you choose for friends can tell you a whole bunch about yourself. Ask yourself these questions:

- ✦ Who are your closest friends, or who do you want to be close friends with?
- ✦ Why do you like being with them?
- ✦ Do you try to be like them? Why?
- ✦ Who do you try to impress?
- ✦ When is it hard being with your friends?
- ✦ Is there a teacher or a coach who seems to get who you really are?
- ✦ Is there an adult you want to be like when you get to be one?
- ✦ Is there someone in your class who reminds you of You?
- ✦ Is there a grown-up besides your parents who you feel comfortable talking to?
- ✦ Do you know a boy who doesn't drive you nuts?

A lot of times we're drawn to people because we see in them what we like about ourselves. The people you admire and feel relaxed with can show you some things about who you are. People you feel shy and awkward with can show you who you aren't! (And remember, that's okay.)

Whew! That's a lot to think about. We're pretty sure you're going to work that hard to see yourself only if you know it's WAY important. Let's check in with God.

Why does God want you to see yourself so clearly? He tells us that himself:

> [God] has saved us and called us to a holy life – not because of anything we have done but because of his own purpose and grace.
> – 2 TIMOTHY 1:9

We didn't make ourselves who we are — God did! The verse says God had a reason, so obviously it's pretty important for us to discover what that is. We can't unless we know ourselves as God made us.

Remember the story of the fig tree that didn't produce any figs? The landowner said to chop it down. The gardener, who knew the garden better, said,

> "Leave it alone for one more year, and I'll dig around it and fertilize it. If it bears fruit next year, fine! If not, then cut it down."
> – LUKE 13:8 - 9

That sounds a little harsh, until you think about it. A fig tree was made to give us figs. The gardener is willing to give it special care, but if it still isn't going to do what it was meant to do, he'll cut it down. That doesn't mean God takes your whole life away! It just means you don't get to do what you were meant to do. You're like a fruit tree — made especially as you are to produce something special for God. If you don't know what kind of tree you are, how can you do that?

The good news is that our Lord (like the gardener) really knows you and is willing to give you special care — show you how to grow into your true self. Don't miss out on God's help because you are a cherry tree busy trying to make apples.

If God went to all the trouble to make every one of the billions of people on the planet unique, doesn't it make sense that God wants you to let everybody see the Holy Spirit working through that special self of yours? Check out what Jesus said in Luke 11:

> "No one lights a lamp and puts it in a place where it will be hidden, or under a bowl. Instead, he [or she] puts it on its stand, so that those who come in may see the light."
> —LUKE 11:33

Jesus was an amazing storyteller, and he used things people were familiar with to help explain things that might be hard to understand. We aren't necessarily acquainted with lighting a lamp and putting it on a stand, so let's try something Jesus might use if he were trying to make his point today:

"Girls, don't become a reclining chair that burps."

Seriously. And he might go on with something like this:

"Imagine this kind of life for your future. The alarm clock rings in the morning. You reach over, pick it up, and throw it across the room. You stumble to the bathroom, and when you see yourself in the mirror, you scare yourself awake with the reflection of a baggy-eyed, frown-faced woman.

"Somehow you get yourself dressed and drag yourself out to your old beat-up car. As soon as you start it up, you remember that you're running on empty. You pray all the way to the gas station that you'll make it. It's the first time you've prayed since ... well, you can't remember when. While you're filling your tank, you realize you're going to be late for work. Again. Sure enough, it's 8:01 when you get there, and your boss glares at you. Man, you hate this job.

"You take your place and you do the same task you do every day, over and over. You immediately break into a sweat. Your stomach growls because you didn't have time for breakfast. You wonder if it's almost lunchtime. You look at your watch.

"It's 8:02.

"Next time you look, it's 8:05. You must look at your watch fifteen hundred times that day, wishing it would be five o'clock. When it finally is, you drive home, drag yourself into the house, flop into your favorite reclining chair, and yell, 'Hey, babe. Order a pizza.'

"Your husband orders a pizza while you pick up the remote and flip through the channels. You watch a rerun of *Friends*. You catch *Wheel of Fortune*. The pizza arrives — greasy and salty and practically cold — and you eat a couple of pieces. It tastes like cardboard. Greasy, salty cardboard.

"You watch a couple of reality shows that are about as much like real life as a cartoon, and the pizza starts to digest. You lean back in your reclining chair, open your mouth, and let a big ol' belch rip through the room. Your husband says, 'Good one.'

"After that, you go to bed, get up the next morning, and do the same thing. Day after day after day . . .

"Is that the kind of life you want, my princesses?" Jesus might say. "Because that's not what the Father had in mind when he created you. God gave you a unique place in this world so you can help people see him. Are you doing that living in a recliner that occasionally erupts with a burp?

"Don't live like that! Get out there and show 'em what you're workin' with: a bursting-with-life spirit with a reason for being here."

You're Good to Go

Ready to find out more about your true self every day? One of the best ways to do that — and it's been used by people (especially women) since paper was invented — is through journaling.

Keeping a journal means writing in a special blank book every day, or at least regularly. It's a way to express your feelings, work out problems, vent about stuff that's driving you bonkers, and describe things that are happening in your life. If you would rather have a tooth pulled — without any novocaine — than write when you don't have to, maybe these will make the idea seem more delicious to you:

* You don't have to worry about spelling, grammar, or punctuation because nobody's ever going to read your journal except you.
* You can write anything you want. Anything.
* You can also draw pictures, write poems and songs, or just plain doodle . . . as long as it's all about you and your life.

❖ You can create your own code if you want to. Use fake names for the people you write about (just in case somebody else — like a nosy big sister — does read it). Use secret words for certain feelings. It's yours, and you can do whatever you want. Really.

Writing in your journal is like having a private clubhouse where you can say anything you want. Even if you write only a couple of lines a day, you'll start to look forward to opening your journal. If that seems weird, write to a pal of your own creation in your journal. Better yet, write to God.

To make your journal even more personal and fun, make your own. You can decorate a plain notebook, but if you want it to be really, really You, try this:

What you'll need:

❖ a piece of 8½" x 11" heavy paper or poster board for the cover
❖ at least twenty sheets of blank filler paper, no bigger than the cover
❖ 30" of ribbon, yarn, or twine
❖ a heavy-duty hole punch
❖ anything you want to decorate it with (glitter, stickers, beads, felt, whatever says YOU!)

What to do:

1. Fold the cover as exactly in half as you can.
2. Mark three places to punch holes along the folded edge (about ½ inch from edge).
3. Punch the three holes in the cover.
4. Fold all the filler paper in half together.

5. Place it inside the cover and mark with a pencil where to punch holes in the paper.
6. Punch the holes in the filler paper. (You might have to do this two or three sheets at a time if your hole punch won't go through all of them.)
7. Put the filler paper inside the cover so the holes line up.
8. Feed your ribbon, yarn, or twine through the center hole until it's halfway through.
9. Bring the end that's on the bottom of the journal up through the top hole.
10. Bring the end that's coming up from the middle hole down through the bottom hole.
11. Bring the end that's now on the bottom of the journal up through the center hole.
12. Both ends should be on the front cover side of the journal. Tie them together in a knot and then make a pretty bow or whatever; you can trim the ends if you want.
13. Decorate the cover so that it's totally YOU.

What to do now:

◎ Keep your journal in a special, hidden place so no one will be tempted to read it. If you think somebody may get into it, you won't be as honest with yourself.

◎ Tell your mom you're keeping a journal and ask her to support you in protecting your privacy.

◎ If parents object to your writing things you don't want them to read, share this chapter with them. Better yet, make each of them a journal. Sometimes it takes a journaler to understand a journaler.

◎ Try to write in your journal at the same time every day. If you can't do that, come as close as you can.

⊚ It's fun to have special pens to write with. Try different colors for different moods or subjects. Or use black for writing and colors for doodling and decorating. This is your special time and place. Make it as totally the Unique You as possible.

⊚ If you just write about what you did during the day, it might get boring once in a while. Most of us don't have thrilling experiences every minute! But if you write about how you feel about something that's going on — or describe one thing that really got you angry, or sad, or overjoyed — it will always be interesting. It's a much better way to get to know yourself.

⊚ It's also fun to write about your hopes and dreams, about how you want things to go — even just the next day. Nothing is too silly to put on paper. And even if it is silly, what's wrong with that?

⊚ If you hate to write, just choose one word for the day, write it really big on your page, and then decorate it. You'll still be thinking about your day and your feelings while you're doing it.

That's What I'm Talkin' About!

I've tried journaling for one week, and it is _____

_____

_____

_____

_____

_____

_____

_____

_____

_____

_____

_____

_____

_____

_____

(You may write your response in your journal if you want to.)

chapter three

What's in
YOUR WAY?

Molly pretended to consult the list of chores on the Galilee Cabin clipboard, but she was really praying. *Father, just let everybody like me, even if I have to tell them they messed up. Please?*

She wasn't totally sure God was going to answer that prayer. Why did she have to be supervisor on the very first day of cabin cleanup anyway? Nobody would hate her if she just had to empty the trash. If she cleaned the toilet, they would probably love her. But being the one who made sure every girl got her chore done ...

Molly sighed and went to Emily.

"Um ... good job getting those dust bunnies," Molly said.

Emily backed out from under a bunk and dragged the dust mop with her. "I know all their names now, trust me."

Molly giggled. "You're too funny," she said as she put a check mark on the chore list.

"Want to hear them?" Emily said.

"Yes!"

Emily pointed her toe at a glob of fuzz in the dust pan. "This one's Harriet. The one next to her is Gladys — "

"I love that!"

"Hello!" Hannah said, head poking out of the bathroom doorway. "I'm ready to be checked off."

"Sorry," Molly muttered.

She hurried to Hannah, who closed the door behind both of them.

"Can you believe how silly that Emily girl is?" she whispered to Molly. "*Naming* clumps of dust? How lame is that?"

Molly cleared her throat and tried to look as sophisticated as Hannah, who was rolling her eyes. Molly rolled hers too.

"It *is* pretty lame," Molly said. "That's like something I did when I was four."

Hannah sniffed. "I don't think I *ever* did it. I was, like, born mature."

Molly nodded soberly and tucked her hair behind one ear. That seemed like a Hannah thing to do.

"So go ahead and check off the showers," Hannah said. "I'm done."

Molly moved toward them, but Hannah caught her arm. "Seriously, I cleaned. You don't even have to look."

Then she smiled sweetly at Molly, and Molly smiled back and checked off "showers" on the list.

"Who's doing toilets?" Molly said.

"Me," said a voice Molly recognized as Lydia's. She was calling from inside a stall. "And it is SO disgusting and foul, I think I'm going to throw up."

"It's not that bad," Hannah whispered to Molly. "All she ever does is complain."

They exchanged eye rolls. Molly peeked inside the stall door to see Lydia standing three feet from the potty and waving a toilet brush over its open lid.

"I can't even stand to touch it," Lydia said. "EWWW!"

"I don't blame you," Molly said in a low voice, although she didn't see so much as a smudge on the toilet. "That's just gross."

"Thank you. Finally somebody gets it." Lydia squinted at Molly. "What's your name again?"

"Molly," she said. "And I SO get it."

Molly checked off Lydia's chore and went to find the girls working outside. She knew they were pretty rowdy, but she could be rowdy ... if she tried.

Why, she wondered, did she feel like a wad of chewing gum right now?

Here's the Deal

You're probably seeing some very cool things in Molly:

She has a sense of humor.

She's basically responsible.

She's friendly.

Uh ... but so far, that's about it. The sad thing we know about Molly is that she tries so hard to please everybody, she can't show the rest of what's awesome in her personality.

She's probably very creative, but she didn't join in the naming of Emily's dust bunnies because Hannah thought it was lame.

She might be a good leader, but we didn't get to see that, because she was afraid Hannah wouldn't like her if she actually checked the showers for herself.

She could even be a great encourager, but nobody will ever know it if she keeps chiming in with Lydia's whining instead of saying what she really thinks: *I don't even see anything on the toilet. Come on, you can SO do this!*

Molly's trying to be funny for Emily, sophisticated for Hannah, rebellious for Lydia, and rowdy for the other girls — and she can't possibly be all those things. When does the real Molly get to come out?

Before we get in her face too much, though, we need to look at ourselves. How many times have you acted like somebody you weren't because you were afraid someone wouldn't like you, or would get mad at you, or would just write you off as silly or lame or as a loser?

You can stop counting now, because if you're like many of us in our early years, you could be there for days remembering all those times! Instead, let's look at some of the common roadblocks that keep girls from moving down the path to their true selves:

- ✿ trying to be perfect
- ✿ what's accepted as cool and what's not
- ✿ what your friends might think
- ✿ what the popular kids might think — whether they're your friends or not
- ✿ what you see on TV and in movies and magazines
- ✿ things you think you need to hide

How can those be barriers to being your real self? Well, what are some of the un-You things you do (or have done)

- ✿ when you're trying to impress somebody?
- ✿ when you want to belong to a particular group, no matter what?
- ✿ when you want attention?
- ✿ when you want to be invisible?

Have you ever

____ told a lie so you'd fit in or wouldn't feel like a weirdo?

____ worn an outfit like everybody else had and felt totally self-conscious the entire time?

____ been at a party where you felt like an alien?

____ not been able to think of anything to say when somebody you really wanted to be friends with started talking to you?

____ snubbed somebody you liked because you were with girls who probably wouldn't accept her?

____ pretended to be fine when you weren't, so nobody would know what you were really feeling?

___ not raised your hand in class, even when you knew the answer, because other kids might think you were a know-it-all or not cool?

There are four main reasons why a girl lets these things happen. Think about whether any of these roadblocks have ever shown up in your mind — and in your actions. Then let's turn each "What If" into a "What Is."

ROADBLOCK #1 — You think you have to be perfect.

When you're just being yourself, you're bound to make mistakes. But here's a news flash: you're going to make even more mistakes if you're always asking . . .

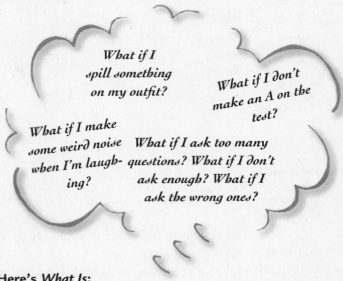

What if I spill something on my outfit?

What if I don't make an A on the test?

What if I make some weird noise when I'm laughing?

What if I ask too many questions? What if I don't ask enough? What if I ask the wrong ones?

Here's *What Is*:

✦ You're not perfect, and you never will be.
✦ Nobody else is perfect either.
✦ You can only be "perfectly yourself," and even that takes courage and practice.

✦ The closest you can get to perfect is to pour out the love ... on God, on other people, and on yourself.

ROADBLOCK #2 — You think your true self isn't good enough.
You go nuts with the questions ...

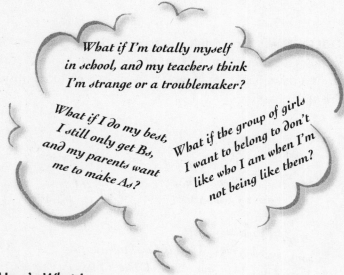

What if I'm totally myself in school, and my teachers think I'm strange or a troublemaker?

What if I do my best, I still only get Bs, and my parents want me to make As?

What if the group of girls I want to belong to don't like who I am when I'm not being like them?

Here's *What Is*:

✦ Everyone is good at something, but nobody is good at everything.
✦ There is at least one good friend — and probably tons of them — for a truly authentic person.
✦ Most people love to be around somebody who's totally real — someone they can trust.
✦ Anybody who rejects you for not being her clone wasn't meant to be your friend right now. At least, not until she discovers *her* real self.

Note: There are certain people who at this point have some control over your life: parents, teachers, and coaches. It may be that you'll have to turn down the volume on your realness when you're around them. Maybe tone down your big laugh or save your mischievous sense of humor for later when you're just with your friends. However, no rule should ever force you to do something you aren't able to do or don't believe in. If you're in that situation, ask your parents or another adult you trust to help you.

ROADBLOCK #3 — You think your true self is way too much.
The questions bug you like a mosquito in the dark . . .

What if I do my best performance in the talent show, and some kids say I'm a show-off?

What if I go all out on a project, and everybody thinks I'm a geek?

What if I make straight As, and my best friend feels bad because she makes Bs?

What if I give the right answers in class so much, the other kids say that I think I'm smarter than they are?

Here's *What Is*:

✦ God gave you a wonderful mind so you can expand it, not shrink it!

✦ You have a job to do with that mind — to make a difference in the world. You can't make that difference if you pretend to be less than you are, so never be a small version of your real self.

✦ There are always people who will be jealous of your talent or your courage to use it. Jealousy can make people say some pretty mean things so they don't have to feel guilty because they aren't using *their* gifts.

✦ Far more people will be inspired by a brave, nothing-held-back performance. Do your thing to the limit and beyond, and you'll give other people the courage to do the same.

✦ What does "geek" mean anyway? The word is usually used by kids who don't understand how amazing it feels to really get into a thing, learn all about it, and share it with other people in an awesome way. Do you want to trade that feeling for their approval? Hey, don't cheat yourself!

IT No matter what people say — "She's just weird," or "She's so goody-goody, she's not any fun," or "She thinks she's all that" — almost everyone at least secretly likes the authentic person. Real, honest, genuine people are so attractive, only the most insecure don't at least admire them from afar. Remember that the more you are like yourself, the more easily you can allow others to be THEMselves.

ROADBLOCK #4—You think you won't be able to keep up if you live honestly. You're always dodging questions like . . .

What if I don't do a sport or an activity every day after school and I miss something (popularity, awards, everybody thinking I'm wonderful at everything)?

What if I don't get the clothes my friends are wearing — even though I don't like them — and they start thinking I'm not cool?

What if I mess up on the test and don't get recommended for honors classes or the gifted program?

What if I don't join in the gossiping — even though I hate talking about people behind their backs — and I don't get invited to the good sleepovers anymore?

Here's *What Is*:

✦ Trying to do it all doesn't make you good at everything. In fact, it doesn't let you be as good as you could be at *some* things—the things you were made to do.

✦ If the clothes you wear make the difference between whether your friends accept you or vote you out of the group ... darlin', they aren't friends.

✦ Those who are gifted in academics (schoolwork) aren't the only ones with special gifts. Use the gifts you have where you can. The rewards will be there.

✦ Being a part of a group should never mean you have to go against what you know is right.

✦ The surest way to fail, and be unhappy, is to try to match everything everybody else is doing.

✦ Find your own rhythm and always walk to it.

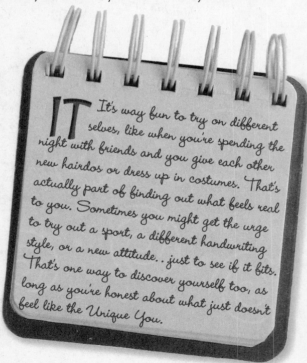

IT It's way fun to try on different selves, like when you're spending the night with friends and you give each other new hairdos or dress up in costumes. That's actually part of finding out what feels real to you. Sometimes you might get the urge to try out a sport, a different handwriting style, or a new attitude.. just to see if it fits. That's one way to discover yourself too, as long as you're honest about what just doesn't feel like the Unique You.

That Is SO Me!

Think about what it feels like when you aren't being yourself and you know it. Sometimes imagining it can make you feel like that right on the spot. Try to make a picture in your mind that matches that feeling. Here are some images other girls have come up with:

"I feel all pointy, like Pinocchio. I can imagine my nose getting sharper with every fakey thing I do."

"I can almost feel myself getting smaller and smaller."

"I think of a puppet, with somebody else pulling the strings."

"It's like I'm in a cave, looking out."

Your mind-picture: _____

_____

Now draw that picture on paper, and keep it with your journal. Look at it every so often and write in your journal about times you've felt like that recently. Whenever you get that feeling, stop and say to yourself: *Oops. I'm not being the Unique Me. What needs to happen?*

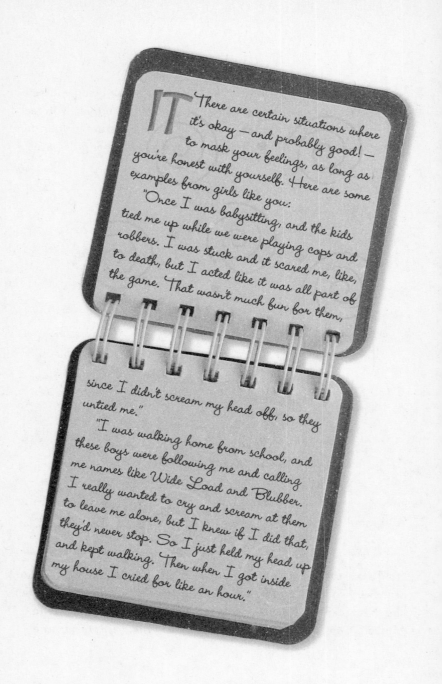

IT There are certain situations where it's okay — and probably good! — to mask your feelings, as long as you're honest with yourself. Here are some examples from girls like you:

"Once I was babysitting, and the kids tied me up while we were playing cops and robbers. I was stuck and it scared me, like, to death, but I acted like it was all part of the game. That wasn't much fun for them, since I didn't scream my head off, so they untied me."

"I was walking home from school, and these boys were following me and calling me names like *Wide Load* and *Blubber*. I really wanted to cry and scream at them to leave me alone, but I knew if I did that, they'd never stop. So I just held my head up and kept walking. Then when I got inside my house I cried for like an hour."

GOT GOD?

Four of the most important things a Christian believes:

1. You are created by God.
2. You are a child of God.
3. You are loved by God.
4. You are accepted by God.

That makes it pretty clear you really can't let roadblocks keep you from being exactly the person God created. If you let anyone or anything be more important than being your God-made self, you're pretty much telling God he doesn't know what he's doing! But the Bible tells us that he does:

> "There's trouble ahead when you live only for the approval of others, saying what flatters them, doing what indulges them. Popularity contests are not truth contests—look how many scoundrel preachers were approved by your ancestors! Your task is to be true, not popular."
> —LUKE 6:26 (THE MESSAGE)

It's not a good idea to live only for the approval of others. Other people can't decide who you ought to be.

"The good man [or woman] brings good things out of the good stored up in his [or her] heart... For out of the overflow of his [or her] heart his [or her] mouth speaks."
—Luke 6:45

All the activities you're involved in, all the sports you play, the great grades you make, how popular you are—none of that makes you who you are. It's what's real in you, deep in your heart.

God doesn't compare us to each other, saying any one of us is a better creation than another. That means we shouldn't compare either. It only makes us cranky. Who you are is good enough for God, so it has to be good enough for you!

Since we live by the Spirit, let us keep in step with the Spirit. Let us not become conceited, provoking and envying each other.
—Galatians 5:25-26

That Is SO Me!

What are your personal roadblocks? Circle all the obstacles below that stand between you and your real self:

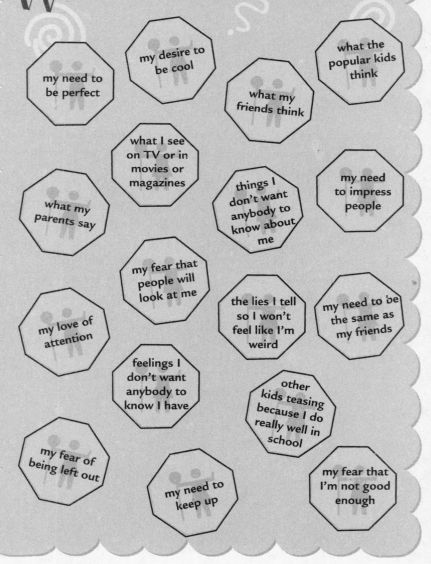

- my need to be perfect
- my desire to be cool
- what my friends think
- what the popular kids think
- what I see on TV or in movies or magazines
- things I don't want anybody to know about me
- my need to impress people
- what my parents say
- my fear that people will look at me
- the lies I tell so I won't feel like I'm weird
- my need to be the same as my friends
- my love of attention
- feelings I don't want anybody to know I have
- other kids teasing because I do really well in school
- my fear of being left out
- my need to keep up
- my fear that I'm not good enough

Draw in this empty space anything else you know is a roadblock for you.

Now number the roadblocks you've circled. Number one will be your biggest obstacle to always being yourself, and your last number will be the smallest obstacle.

Just knowing what's standing in the way — and how big it is to you — will help you be aware of how much you hide the real You. It's the first step in getting the barrier out of the way.

There are more steps, which we're going to talk about in the rest of our chapters. Meanwhile, write your roadblocks in your journal, and check each time you do your journaling to see if you've made progress in jumping over them.

For I am convinced that... [nothing] ... will be able to separate us from the love of God that is in Christ Jesus our Lord.
— ROMANS 8:38-39

IT It's almost impossible to completely destroy the barriers that keep you from doing your natural thing. There will always be jealous kids, demanding parents, and people who tease or say mean things. Even your own secret fears will hang around in the back of your mind. But just because they're there doesn't mean you can't get past them. That's what the rest of this book is about.

You're Good to Go

Can you think of one thing you like to do that none of your friends like to do — or that you've never told them about? Maybe it's

- ❖ listening to music that isn't popular;
- ❖ reading your favorite book for the fiftieth time;
- ❖ practicing your basketball free throw, or your split, or your juggling;
- ❖ concocting something in the kitchen;
- ❖ hiding in the attic;
- ❖ planting petunias;

❖ designing a whole wardrobe; or
❖ playing with finger paints, watercolors, or modeling clay.

Whatever it is, write it here: _____
_____

Now, make an appointment with yourself to do that little thing.

What you'll need:

❖ one hour to yourself this week
❖ whatever things you'll have to have (paints, your CD player, recipe ingredients)

What to do:

❖ Try not to think about what your friends would say or whether your brother will tease you.
❖ Just enjoy doing what is totally and uniquely your thing.
❖ Savor every minute as if you were licking your favorite ice cream. Being you is a delicious experience!

What this tells you:

❖ how you enjoy your own company
❖ how natural it feels to be YOU, so you'll remember next time you're acting unnatural
❖ what else you might enjoy doing next time

What to do now:

◎ If you can, have an appointment with yourself once a week.

◎ Have fun getting to know YOU!

That's What I'm Talkin' About!

When I spent a whole hour just being me, it was _____

_____

_____

_____

_____

_____

_____

_____

_____

_____

_____

_____

_____

_____

_____

_____

_____

chapter four

Talkin' Trash —
TALKIN' TRUTH!

M olly lay still as a doll, breathing deeply and evenly. She
even let out a fake snore.

But Hannah poked her with a foot and whispered,
"We know you're not really asleep, Molly."

"Come on, Mol'," Lydia whispered from the other side. "You
have to do this with us."

Somebody — probably one of the rowdy girls — pitched a
pillow at Molly from across the room. As Molly sat up in bed, her
mouth was already going dry.

"Do what with you?" she said with mock sleepiness —
although she knew exactly what. The rest of the cabin had been
talking — ever since lights-out — about sneaking out and scaring
the boys down in the Nazareth and Canaan Cabins. Her heart
had pounded through the whole discussion.

"We need your ideas," Emily said. "You're the creative one."

"And you know you want to get those boys as much as we
do," Hannah said. She gave Molly another foot poke. "You're the
most boy crazy of any of us."

"Besides," Lydia said. "If we get caught, you'll be able to
explain it all to the adults, because they always listen to you. You
totally know how to fake them out."

Somebody from the Rowdy Girls group let out a hoot. "We're not gonna get caught! Molly's the toughest girl in this cabin — she can lead us so nobody'll ever know."

"Huddle up!" Hannah whispered hoarsely.

Suddenly everybody in the cabin was around Molly's bed, watching her as if she already had a plan in mind.

But the only thing in her head was panicked screams. *Why do I have to be the leader? I'm not all that stuff they think I am!*

She wanted to say, "We shouldn't do this. We'll get in SO much trouble."

But the way they were looking at her, all expectant, like she was the smartest girl on the planet — and the most creative — and the toughest — and the boy-craziest — how could she say no?

They'll all figure out I'm not what they think I am. They'll hate me for the whole rest of camp!

The thought of those first few lonely days before she'd figured out how to get her cabin mates to like her brought the sick feeling back to Molly's stomach.

"O-kay," she said slowly. And then she didn't have a clue what to say next.

Molly is definitely tangled up in a situation. And you've probably figured out by now that she wove the web herself by trying to be what everybody else wanted her to be.

Yeah, that's pretty much what happens when you try to be a chameleon. But Molly doesn't—and you don't—have to act like a little lizard that changes color to blend in with the background. Who wants to be a reptile anyway?

You *can* be liked for who you are. You're getting to know yourself better and are starting to leap over your roadblocks. So how about we learn how to talk the truth about you?

You can start by erasing three "trash" phrases from your vocabulary that might be littering up your journey. Then you can begin replacing these phrases with true ones:

Piece of Trash #1 — "I'm so _____."
Fill in the line with a familiar put-down of yourself. Here are some examples:

> "I am SO fat."
> "I'm so totally dumb in math."
> "I'm so spastic at sports."
> "I SO have the biggest mouth in life."
> "I so hate my laugh. I sound like a pig."
> "I'm so lame at art."
> "I'm so much of a loser!"

Then STOP talking to yourself that way. You wouldn't say those things to your friends, so don't say them to yourself! Du-uh!

Try turning them upside down in your mind — from downers to uppers:

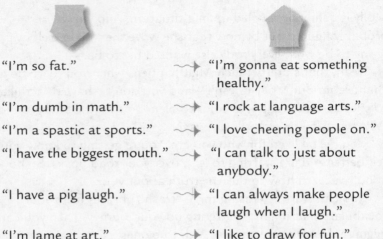

"I'm so fat." ⟿ "I'm gonna eat something healthy."

"I'm dumb in math." ⟿ "I rock at language arts."

"I'm a spastic at sports." ⟿ "I love cheering people on."

"I have the biggest mouth." ⟿ "I can talk to just about anybody."

"I have a pig laugh." ⟿ "I can always make people laugh when I laugh."

"I'm lame at art." ⟿ "I like to draw for fun."

"I'm a loser." ⟿ "Everyone's a winner at something."

When you can't say anything nice about yourself, say something nice about somebody else:

("I'm so fat.") "She looks so cute in that outfit."

("I'm dumb in math.") "You are, like, the class math whiz."

Do NOT add an insult to yourself when you compliment someone else: "She looks so cute in that outfit. I wish I were skinny like her."

DO add a gentle request for help: "You are, like, the class math whiz. Could you help me with the homework?"

That way, you're still learning how to speak kindly to other people, and you'll slowly start being gentler with yourself too.

Piece of Trash #2 — "I can't _____**."** Fill in the line with something you haven't even tried very hard to do. Yeah, we're talking about . . .

"I can't go to a party where I don't know anybody."

"I can't talk in front of people."

"I can't learn to . . . (swim, dance, ski, ice-skate, bake brownies, do a cartwheel, eat a lobster . . .)"

"I can't get along with my sister/brother."

"I can't go to school when my friends are mad at me."

Everybody gets freaked out sometimes when there's something new to try—from going to a different school to eating sushi for the first time. But nobody knows if she can do it until she gives it an honest effort. If it turns out you really can't do it, you'll know you need some more help (like in a school subject or an important relationship), or you'll discover that it really isn't your thing (like in a sport or one of the arts). Either way, you'll have the satisfaction of knowing you tried, and that can really build your confidence in yourself. Besides, most of the time, you'll discover you really CAN do it. So instead of saying, *"I can't,"* say, *"I'll try."*

IT Hating anything about your true self makes you more false, not more real. If you hate it, you're going to try to cover it up and try to be something else. If you look at it as a challenge or just hug it, then you can keep going toward the Unique You.

"I don't like going to parties where I don't know anybody, but I can try to make some new friends at this one."

"I get shy talking in front of people, but I can try doing my report for just my family before I have to do it in school."

"I don't know how to swim yet, but I'll try taking lessons."

"My little brother drives me nuts, but I'm gonna try being really nice to him for a week and see what happens." (Or, "I'll try not to smack him for at least three days.")

"My friends at school are all mad at me, but I'm going to try to make up."

IT We all have limits on what we can do, so it's good to start discovering those too. Limits are things like how much sleep your body requires, how much alone time you need, how much frustration you can take before you blow, and how you learn best. Talk to your parents about that. They've been discovering your natural limits since you were born, and they can help you make good choices in how you go at the things you want to try.

Piece of Trash #3 — "If only_____." We all tend to say that when we want something to be different:

"If only I weren't bigger than everyone else in my whole entire class."
"If only I were funnier."
"If only I didn't get my feelings hurt so easy."
"If only I were the best at something . . . anything!"

Before you say *if only* again, decide whether that's something you can change, or something you need to just accept.

You can't change your height or your nose or the shape of your face. And why would you want to? That's what you look like, not who you are. If you want to look your best, read *The Beauty Lab*, but do it so you'll feel beautiful inside and out, not so other people will like you.

You can't change the qualities you were born with, but you can make them shine. You might not be funny, but who says you have to be? Polish up your knack for encouraging people, or for getting them to talk about themselves, or for making them see they're about to do something stupid.

Everyone can be her own personal best at something. Enough with the competition, already! There might be only one Olympic gold medal for figure skating, but there are millions of girls out there getting better at it every day and loving it. It's the same for anything you do. Forget about awards and medals, and be the best YOU!

So instead of saying, *"If only,"* start saying, *"I always."*

"I always try to look exactly like me."
"I always give my friends the best of who I am (or at least I try to)."
"I always try to see both sides before I decide that somebody meant to hurt my feelings."
"I always look for ways to improve at the things I have to do and the things I love to do."

That Is SO Me!

It's time to check out your own trash talking — just so you can watch out for them in your thoughts and in your talk. It's so much easier to keep the trash out when you know what it is! Circle every trash-talkin' thing that gets hung up in your mind. Write in your own if it is missing here.

What negative things do you say "I'm so_____" about?

my height   my weight   my face

my schoolwork   my athletic ability   my hair   my popularity

how I get along with people   how outgoing I am   my artistic talent   my laugh

how I talk

Anything else? _____

What do you say "I can't_____" about?

sports   exercise   outdoor activities

subjects in school   how I organize my schoolwork   how I behave in school   how I get along with teachers

how I get along with other kids   how I get along with my family   my appearance

chores   artistic activities

Anything else? _____

What negative things do you say "If only _____" about?

money   material stuff   my room

school subjects   teachers   the school day

my family   my hobbies

sports   kids at school

my body

pets   church

my appearance   friends   artistic activities

Anything else? _____

Look at the areas of your life you've circled above. Make a list in your journal of the **exact** things you tell yourself about each one. Examples:

★ popularity—"I'm so outside the cool kids' group."
★ how I organize my schoolwork—"I can't ever find anything. I'm just a ditz."
★ teachers—"If only I were smarter. Then Mrs. So-and-So would like me."

Now you can really sweep out that trash and replace it with the truth:

★ "I'm cool enough to start my own group of friends."
★ "I can get Mrs. So-and-So to help me get organized—and while I'm at it, I can get help with math too."

You won't be able to snap your fingers and immediately become a truth teller, especially when just about everyone you know goes around saying, "I am so—," "I can't—," and "If only—." But it will help to remember how God talks about you. After all . . .

> My dear children, let's not just talk about love; let's practice real love. This is the only way we'll know we're living truly, living in God's reality. It's also the way to shut down debilitating self-criticism, even when there is something to it. For God is greater than our worried hearts and knows more about us that we do ourselves.
> —1 John 3:19 (The Message)

It says here that we can be at rest when we realize God knows better than the ugly, hateful things we say about ourselves. This is what *he* says:

> "You are always with me, and everything I have is yours."
> —Luke 15:31

In the story Jesus told about the prodigal son, the father said those words to the son who *didn't* take off and try to do his own thing. The father represents God, who says that same thing to you. It comes not so much in words as in the feeling of realness when you're being who God made you to be. In the times when you're being natural and true to yourself, you feel strong, don't you? That's the presence of God. You're with him, and everything he has is yours. Now, that's a sweet thing to say!

> While he was still a long way off, his father saw him and was filled with compassion for him; he ran to his son, threw his arms around him and kissed him.
> —LUKE 15:20

In the very same story, when the son who wasted all his money and time comes home, Jesus says that God loves us even when we do mess up. He celebrates when we realize we've been morons and go back to him. He (God) says to the other son, who's annoyed because he never got a party for being good,

> "We had to celebrate and be glad, because this brother of yours was dead and is alive again; he was lost and is found."
> —LUKE 15:32

He doesn't say, "Your brother's so irresponsible," or "He can't handle money," or "If only he were more like you." He sees him as his high-energy, free-spirit son who's ready to learn to use all that in good ways. He sees the real You too, and welcomes you when you "come home" to your true self.

Part of "coming home" is in speaking only the truth to yourself: that you are God's precious work-in-progress. There's no room in that for talking trash about your sweet self.

You're Good to Go

One of the best things you can do to stop thinking and talking trash about yourself is to be grateful for everything that is wonderful about you and your life. You can get a start on that by making and filling a *treasure chest*.

What you'll need:

❖ A box — A shoebox is fine. If you want to really go all out, ask your mom if you can use that old toy box or an empty bin (the kind she stores the Christmas decorations in), but think about where you're going to keep it first!
❖ Decorative items — Use anything you want to decorate it the way you imagine your perfect treasure chest to look. It doesn't have to become something out of *Pirates of the Caribbean* if your idea is more funky or artsy or sleek.

What to do:

❖ Decorate your box until it really says You.
❖ Fill it with things that represent what's great about you and your life. Here are some ideas:

  — pictures of you with friends and family, or shots that capture your special moods
  — artwork you've done
  — stories you've written
  — notes and cards from people expressing their love for you

- "souvenirs" of your activities (last year's soccer cleats, dance recital programs, a piece from your shell collection ...)
- reminders of special occasions
- anything that says something positive about you (your favorite flower pressed into your most-loved book, a miniature soccer ball, your name spelled out in sequins on paper ...)

❖ Write a letter to yourself. Tell yourself everything you appreciate about you. Remind yourself of all the things you love about your life. Promise yourself you'll try never to put any of that down or wish you were more or had more. Decorate a copy of the letter to match You and keep it in your treasure chest.

What this tells you:

- ❖ what a treasure your life is
- ❖ how thankful you can be for just being who you are
- ❖ what's really important to you
- ❖ how important you are to God

What to do now:

◎ Add to your treasure chest when you discover something new about yourself. It's going to happen a lot!

◎ Go to your treasure chest as often as you like, but especially when you find yourself having a bad case of the "If only's," the "I'm so's," or the "I can'ts." It will help you remember that's trash talk, and you'll soon be talking truth and treasure to yourself. After all, we are most ourselves when we love the most.

That's What I'm Talkin' About!

While I was filling my treasure chest, I felt _____

_____

_____

_____

_____

_____

_____

_____

_____

_____

_____

_____

_____

_____

_____

_____

chapter five

Being You—
BEING HER

Molly could barely hold back the tears as she stood, trembling, in front of Jerry. He was ONLY the head of the whole camp. He could send her and everybody else in Galilee Cabin home in disgrace any minute now. Who wouldn't want to cry?

Well, actually, Hannah, Molly noticed. She stood next to Molly with her arms folded and her chin stuck out, almost as if she were daring Jerry to accuse her of being out after lights-out. Even though he had *caught* them all hiding in the bushes outside the boys' cabin.

Hannah doesn't even care what he thinks, Molly said to herself. *I wish I could be like that.*

On the other side of her, Emily was making noises like she was holding back the hiccups, but Molly knew better. Emily could hardly keep from giggling. Right then, Molly would gladly have traded her choked-back sobs for Emily's everything's-so-funny attitude.

"Well?" Jerry said. He lowered his eyebrows at the girls. "Anybody have an explanation?"

Lydia gave a sigh that seemed way dramatic to Molly and flashed Jerry a smile as bright as a pair of headlights.

"We just lost our heads," she said. "You know how girls are."

Molly had never seen anybody bat her eyelashes before, but she was pretty sure that was what Lydia was doing. Molly looked at Jerry. He put his hand over his mouth, but his eyes twinkled.

She's actually gonna get away with that! Molly thought. *If I tried that —*

Well, she never would. She didn't know how to act all flirty like Lydia, although at the moment she sure wished she could.

She couldn't be cool like Hannah or laugh it off like Emily either.

Suddenly it hit Molly that trying to be like them was the reason she was standing here in the first place. If she'd done what *she* wanted to do, she'd still be in her bunk. Slowly she raised her hand. Jerry nodded at her.

"The truth is," Molly said, "somebody got the idea to scare the boys — "

Hannah jabbed her — hard — in the ribs. But Molly kept going. She even cried while she poured out the truth. It was the only thing she knew to do.

Yea, Molly! She's finally getting it!

Of course, she had to be on the verge of being tossed out of camp before she figured out that the best thing to be is who you are. Going down the Comparison Dead End was what got her all mixed up to begin with.

You know the one:

"I'm not as smart as she is."

"She's way cuter than I am."

"I wish I could be popular like her."

"I hate that she's so much better at softball than I am."

"Next to hers, my drawings look like a three-year-old did them."

"Why couldn't I have been the funny one in the family like my sister? Everybody loves HER."

And that's only the first stretch in the Comparison Dead End. The next thing you know, you've rounded the next curve and you're saying,

"Well, at least I'm not a stuck-up snob about my grades like she is."

"I may not be as cute, but I think I'm way nicer."

"Who wants to be popular anyway? She just thinks she's all that."

You get the idea. If you slip around the final bend, you'll hear yourself saying, "Hey, you guys! I heard that she makes As by cheating. I think I might have even seen her do it."

By the time you get to that point, you're so far away from yourself, you can't find your way back. How does that happen?

You focus so much on what you aren't, you don't think about what you are — just You. Not you compared to everybody else.

It's hard to live with thinking you're less than other people, so you find ways to bring them down with you. Since that isn't the way you really want to act, you aren't being yourself.

But when you don't feel better, you have to bring your friends into it with you. Maybe you'll feel less "inferior" if you can make that "superior" person miserable. It doesn't work, because deep inside, you really hate what you're doing — becoming something you're not.

EWW, huh? So how do you stop doing that? It isn't easy, because the world we live in measures people against each other all the time.

- ✿ The Olympics compares athletes to see who's the best in the world.
- ✿ Every sport has its version of the Super Bowl to see who the champions are.
- ✿ Beauty pageants determine who's the prettiest.
- ✿ You probably know who the smartest kid in your class is.

Competition can be fun, and it challenges people to do their very best. But it isn't meant to tell people whether they're better or worse than somebody else. And it SURE isn't something you should be doing in everyday situations. What is the point of asking yourself these questions:

Do my parents love me as much as they do the other kids?
Am I smarter or dumber than the rest of my class?
Is my artwork the best of anybody I know?
Do I get as much attention in class as my best friend?
Do I get invited to as many parties as the "cool girls"?
Do I dance better than the rest of the girls in my group?

Instead, ask yourself, WHO CARES? Seriously. Does it matter whether you're smarter, more talented, more popular, more talented, or more loved than anybody else on the planet?

Hello! No! What matters is that

- ✿ you are as loving to your family as YOU can be.
- ✿ you do YOUR best in school.
- ✿ you develop your talents the best YOU can.
- ✿ you treat other people the way YOU want to be treated.
- ✿ you ask for help when YOU need it.
- ✿ you keep trying when YOU make a mistake.

The only person you should be comparing yourself to is the person you were yesterday. Are you just a little more real today? That's what makes it the Unique You adventure!

That Is SO Me!

Who do you compare yourself to? Answer each of these questions honestly. You can write NO or NOBODY if that's your true answer.

Who's the smartest kid in your class? _____

Do you think you're smarter or "dumber" than him/her? _____

Does that make you want to either give up or compete with him/her for grades (even in secret)? _____

Who's the best girl athlete in your school? _____

Do you wish you could be as good as she is? _____

Does her ability make you want to give up or "beat" her, even if she's on your team? _____

What's your best talent? _____

Do you know somebody your age who you think is more talented than you are at that? _____

Does her talent make you want to either give up or take her place from her? _____

Who's the most popular girl you know? _____

Do you think she's more likable than you are? _____

Does her popularity make you feel like a nobody or like taking her title as Miss Popularity? _____

Who do you think is your teacher's "pet"? _____

Does seeing her do her "pet" thing make you want to either misbehave or steal her position? _____

Look over your answers. If you have any NOs or NOBODYs, good for you. You don't always take the Comparison Dead End, and we hope you'll go there less and less. Wherever you don't have NO or NOBODY, think about what you've reported and have a big ol' belly laugh. Really. WHAT were you thinking, huh? Give yourself a break from figuring out where you stand next to everyone else. That's way less fun than just being the best you can be.

There's more to it than feeling better about yourself too.
The Comparison Dead End can keep you away from important
truths about your life. Truths that come from God.

> For you [God] created my inmost being;
>   you knit me together in my mother's womb.
> I praise you because I am fearfully and wonderfully made;
>   your works are wonderful,
>   I know that full well.
> My frame was not hidden from you
>   when I was made in the secret place.
> When I was woven together in the depths of the earth,
>   your eyes saw my unformed body.
> All the days ordained for me
>   were written in your book
>   before one of them came to be.
>   – PSALM 139:13-16

You were custom-designed. Tailor-made. Handcrafted. Set
up for a purpose nobody else has. Doesn't it make sense—if God
has a unique, one-of-a-kind plan for your life, which he decided
before he even *started* making you—that
he gave you the right personality to
carry it out? And that personality
is different from everyone else's,
because each other person has a
unique plan too. There is, then,
no "model person" everybody is
supposed to copy!

Oh, and about that plan:

> "For I know the plans
> I have for you," declares
> the LORD, "plans to prosper you
> and not to harm you, plans to
> give you hope and a future."
> – JEREMIAH 29:11

Why miss out on what God has in store for you while you're trying to get in on his plan for somebody else? Your plans are the best — for YOU!

IT The same goes for comparing yourself to other people and deciding you're BETTER than they are! You know, "I'm not as pretty, but I'm WAY smarter." Jesus taught us about that in the story about the Pharisee who prayed, "God, I thank you that I am not like other [people]" (Luke 18:11). If, like him, you go around with your nose in the air, you might end up falling flat on your face. Be content with who you are, Jesus tells us — no more, no less. After all, God thought the real You was worth dying for.

That Is SO Me!

One sure way to avoid getting trapped in the Comparison Dead End is to have so much fun being YOU, it seems absolutely ridiculous to wonder what it's like to be somebody else. Try this quiz just for giggles. It's even more of a riot when you do it with friends. (It's good sleepover material.)

Choose one of the answers in each category that best fits your real self, or write your own idea in the space provided. Choose the one that is like you in some way. (For example, I'm helpful like a pickup truck.)

If I were a car, I'd be a _____.
    cherry-red Camaro   yellow pickup truck
    silver Lexus   white SUV

If I were a dog, I'd be a _____.
    golden retriever   miniature poodle
    Doberman pinscher   beagle

If I were a color, I'd be _____.
    pink   red   yellow   green

If I were a song, I'd be _____.
    rock   country   rap   opera

If I were a restaurant, I'd be _____.
    a fast-food burger stop   a dinner house with tablecloths
    a health-food shop   a sushi bar

If I were a couch, I'd be _____.
    genuine leather   a sectional with tons of pillows
    white brocade   an antique

If I were a vacation, I'd be _____.
    a hike in the Rockies   a cruise in the Caribbean
    a week in a theme park   a sightseeing tour in Europe

Now, put them all together, and see if what you've chosen describes the real You.

Here's Molly's example:

I'm Molly Ann McPherson, and I'm as practical and dependable as an SUV. I'm the beagle who gets the job done but who loves to play. I'm true blue, like the chorus to your favorite country song, like your favorite burger joint. You can lean on me like a comfy sofa, and trust me because I'm a familiar walk in the woods. That's me, Molly Ann McPherson. Nice to meet you.

You don't have to write yours out if you don't want to, but be sure to share it with the people who know you well. Challenge them to take the quiz too. How fun to discover why the poodle in you doesn't always get along with the Doberman in your brother! And how you and your best friend can double the fun together, because she's Disneyland and you're a hike in the Rockies!

Now that you're seeing how much fun it is to be You, it's safe for you to look at the difference between wanting to BE other people and wanting to be LIKE them in some way.

Let's say there's an older girl, perhaps a friend of your big sister, who you really admire. Maybe you like the way she talks to you, like you're one of the girls instead of an annoying little pest. And maybe you've noticed how she's always ready to try something new, even your mom's brussels sprouts casserole. And she can be honest but not hurt people's feelings. You'd like to be like her someday.

That doesn't mean you want to trade yourself in for a carbon copy of that girl. She just behaves in a way that appeals to you, and there is nothing wrong with wanting to act that way too. In fact, it's very *right*, because what you admire in her is what God wants to see in all of us: kindness, confidence, and honesty.

Think about one person you look up to and respect, even among kids your own age. What is it about her (or him) that makes you think she (or he) is awesome? Could it be that she

★ doesn't get mad easily;
★ treats every person like that person is worth a lot;
★ seems happy with what she has;
★ doesn't brag;
★ is always sharing with people;
★ encourages everyone;
★ makes people smile instead of frown;
★ feels sad when something bad happens to someone, even someone she's not friends with;
★ celebrates with people instead of being jealous of them;
★ stands up for her friends;
★ is a person people can trust;
★ keeps a positive attitude instead of whining; and
★ doesn't give up easily?

She might be quiet or the class clown but still have those qualities. She might be a soccer player or a bookworm and be like that just the same. It's not about her personality or her clothes or the awards she has hanging up in her room. It's about the way she *loves* people. And it's a good thing to want to love the way she does. In fact, that's the one way God wants all of us to be the same.

GOT GOD?

Evidently the people in a town called Corinth, back in the early days of Christianity, were all trapped in the Comparison Dead End. They were arguing. Who was the best at speaking in tongues? Why did this guy have the gift of prophecy and this guy didn't? That lady could heal a sick person with her faith, but that one, now, she could move mountains. One person sold half of what he owned for the poor, so the next guy sold *everything* . . .

It was a mess, so Paul wrote a letter telling them to get out of that dead end. They all had certain gifts, and they ought to be using them for the good of the whole community. He said it didn't matter how they used their talents, because if they didn't ALL start loving each other the way Jesus loved people, they would have nothing.

He explained that God wanted them ALL to be the SAME in the way they loved:

Love is patient, love is kind.
It does not envy, it does not boast, it is not proud.
It is not rude, it is not self-seeking, it is not easily angered,
    it keeps no record of wrongs.
Love does not delight in evil but rejoices with the truth.
It always protects, always trusts, always hopes, always perseveres.
                                    —1 CORINTHIANS 13:4-7

When you discover someone who loves that way, that person can be a *role model* for you. By watching that person, you can learn how to express love like that too. You aren't copying her. You're being influenced by her. Need some examples?

This is looking to someone as a role model: Your teacher says something positive to every student coming into the room in the mornings. You do the same thing with the people who sit around you. Then you start doing it at home at breakfast.

This is trying to be someone else: Your best friend has a funny, snorty laugh that everybody likes. You practice for hours trying to laugh the same way.

This is looking to someone as a role model: The cool teenage girl who babysits for you and your siblings never yells at your little brother, who has been known to bring past babysitters to tears. She plays Superman with him, calls him pal, and smiles at him a lot. You decide to be nicer to him instead of screaming at him every time he comes into your room.

This is trying to be someone else: The girl everybody seems to like tells jokes at lunch every day. You memorize a bunch to share at the table and begin to tell one as soon as she sits down.

There are different kinds of gifts, but the same Spirit.
– 1 CORINTHIANS 12:4

You're Good to Go

It makes a lot of sense at this point for you to make an *admiration list*, giving the names of people you know who have the qualities we talked about in "Got God?"

What you'll need:

- ✦ a piece of the very coolest paper you can find
- ✦ your favorite pens and markers
- ✦ stickers, glitter, stencils for decorating your list (optional)

What to do:

- ✦ Write the names of all the people you admire who love the way God wants us to.
- ✦ Decorate it if you want to.
- ✦ Leave room for more names as you discover new people.

What this tells you:

- ✦ what qualities you want to work on in yourself
- ✦ who you want to spend time with

What to do now:

- ◎ You might want to keep it with your journal so you can look at it often and see how wonderfully well those same qualities are growing in you.

- ◎ Love your true self even more.

That's What I'm Talkin' About!

When I finished my admiration list, I discovered that the person I admire most in this whole world is _____, and that really says something about me. (You can write your response in your journal if you want to.)

chapter six

Just
DO IT!

Molly had the squirmy feeling that somebody was looking at her. She glanced up from the treasure chest she was painting in the camp craft shop. Somebody *was* staring at her. Hannah. With eyes as hard as two bullets.

"You know you're the whole reason we don't get to go to the bonfire on the beach tonight, don't you?" Hannah said.

It was Molly's turn to stare. "*What* are you talking about?" she said.

Lydia slapped down her paintbrush, splattering blossom blue all over the table. "If you hadn't confessed to Jerry in, like, the first seven seconds," she whined, "I could have just smiled our way out of it."

Hannah grunted. "But no, you had to go and be all responsible."

"Dude — I didn't think you'd do that," said one of the rowdy girls at the other end of the table. She pulled back her loaded paintbrush as if she were going to fling roaring red right at Molly. Only a frown from the arts and crafts lady stopped her.

The only person at the table who wasn't glaring at Molly was Emily. She was chewing on the tip of her paintbrush handle and staring at her unpainted treasure chest.

She looks as miserable as I feel, Molly thought.

Ever since last night when Molly had told Jerry the truth about their out-of-the-cabin escapade, the rest of the girls in the cabin had been treating Molly like she was poison ivy. All except Emily, who acted like she *had* a case of it. She seemed squirmy and itchy, and she kept ducking her head, as if she didn't want anyone to see her.

Am I acting like that? Molly wondered. *Like I'm the only one who's done anything wrong?*

Yes, she'd snuck out of the cabin with everyone else. But when they'd gotten caught, they all waited for Molly to do the explaining to Jerry.

It wasn't until after she told him the truth — that they'd broken the rule and they didn't have an excuse — that she realized the other girls had been expecting her to make up a "creative story." Or lead them like a tough-girl gang. Or sweet-talk Jerry into letting them off.

Molly sat back and studied the big heart she'd painted on her treasure chest.

We're making these so we can fill them with things that represent our true selves, she told herself. And so far she planned to fill it with the journal she'd started here at camp, the totally cool shell she'd found on the beach during quiet time, and her admiration list. The first person on that list was Jerry himself, because he was fair and honest ... like she wanted to be.

"Aren't you even going to say you're sorry?" Lydia said.

Molly slowly shook her head. "No," she said, "because I'm *not* sorry. I couldn't make up a story or act like a tough chick or be all flirty, 'cause none of that's me."

"Huh?" somebody from the other end said.

"I had to be honest," Molly said. "*That's* me."

Hannah rolled her eyes. "Well, don't you just think you're all that."

"No, she doesn't."

They all turned to blink at Emily. For the first time that day, she was looking at Molly. Her usually sparkly, mischievous eyes were round and serious.

"I should have done what you did, Molly," Emily said. "I'm gonna put you at the top of my admiration list."

Here's the Deal

You go, Molly! She's discovered that trying to be like the other girls so they would like her didn't make them like her at all. Only when she acted like Molly did she make her first for-real friend at camp. At the same time, she learned something WAY important about herself—that she's honest and responsible and very brave.

How did she figure that out? By doing it! You can learn about yourself not only from things like journaling and changing the way you talk to You, but from *doing*

* what you're taught is right, even if it isn't fun.
* what you know is loving, even if it isn't easy.
* what you see is needed, even if you'd WAY rather be doing something else.
* what you could do if you tried a little harder, even if it stretches you.
* what really matters to you, even if it doesn't matter to any of your friends.
* what God seems to be telling you, even if it wasn't what you had planned.

You can navigate your way into the best version of You. And it isn't complicated. Here are some "travel guides" to take with you as you move into the most challenging part of the Unique You adventure:

TRAVEL GUIDE #1 — Accept yourself each day. (You've got that part, right?) But don't settle for just staying as you are today if it's in your power tomorrow to be just a little better.

> "I'm not naturally good at math, but if I spent more time on my homework, I could probably do better."
>
> "I'm shy, just like my mom, but if I asked that one girl about her horse, I bet she'd talk to me. It would even be okay if my face turned all red."

TRAVEL GUIDE #2 — Try one new thing every day. It doesn't have to be big.

> "I'll say hi to that girl at school I've never spoken to before."
>
> "I'm going to use one of our vocabulary words today and see if anybody notices."
>
> "I think I'll try pickles on my peanut butter sandwich instead of jelly."
>
> "Here goes — two cartwheels in a row instead of just one."

TRAVEL GUIDE #3 — Let go of things that don't "fit" anymore. If it's not You, move on to something else.

> "I'm sick of gossiping with my usual crowd at lunch. I'm going to sit with my soccer friends and talk about the game instead."
>
> "I don't want to fight with my brother over the remote anymore. Let him watch what he wants. I'd rather read anyway."
>
> "I've turned out to be too tall for competing in gymnastics. I think I'll learn to play basketball."

TRAVEL GUIDE #4 — Refuse to let your mistakes make you afraid to keep going.

> "I really blew that test. My dad'll be disappointed in my grade, but I'm going to ask him for help tonight anyway."
>
> "She's really mad at me for what I said. She'll probably scream at me when I go talk to her. But I want to say I'm sorry and see if we can still be friends."
>
> "I bruised my knee big-time when I fell on my skates, but I know what I did wrong. I'm ready to go for it again."
>
> "It'll be hard to get that teacher to trust me after she caught me cheating, but I have to show her that I've learned my lesson — show her AND me!"

TRAVEL GUIDE #5 — Learn as much as you can about Jesus and how he treated people. Try to do as he would do, the way you would with any person you admire.

> "They teach that in Sunday school. I'm going to pay more attention instead of writing notes to my best friend during class!"
>
> "Maybe our moms could start a girls' Bible study after school on Wednesdays."
>
> "I can talk to Jesus anytime I want to in my own mind. I might not hear an out-loud answer, but I know he's listening."
>
> "I'll ask my mom if she'll buy me that cool devotional book for girls I saw at the bookstore. It tells you what to read in the Bible every day."

With those travel guides "packed," you're ready for the road. And who better to provide directions than God himself?

GOT GOD?

It's possible to see the Gospels—the four stories of Jesus' life and teachings in the Bible—as a map to your true self.

Start here:

> "If anyone would come after me, he [or she] must deny himself [or herself] and take up his cross daily and follow me."
>
> —LUKE 9:23

What that means:

Jesus tells us to give up our false selves—all the stuff that isn't who we were created to be—and focus on what he wants us to be and do. And we've already learned that what he wants for us is to be who we truly are.

How to do that:

Pray. Really talk to him. Learn as much as you can about him. Use what you've learned when you're making decisions and solving problems. You'll begin to know what God wants you to do.

> "It's who you are and the way you live that count before God. Your worship must engage your spirit in the pursuit of truth. That's the kind of people the Father is out looking for: those who are simply and honestly themselves before him in their worship."
>
> —JOHN 4:23-24 (THE MESSAGE)

What that means:

If you show God that you love him in honest, real ways, you'll have more of his spirit in you. What could be more real than that?

How to do that:

Sing like you mean it. Pray your true thoughts. Stop and wonder about the world God has made, and thank him for it. Express your love for him however you want to when it bubbles up in you—and don't ever be embarrassed to do that.

"Don't set people up as experts over your life, letting them tell you what to do. Save that authority for God; let him tell you what to do … Do you want to stand out? Then step down. Be a servant. If you puff yourself up, you'll get the wind knocked out of you. But if you're content to simply be yourself, your life will count for plenty."
— MATTHEW 23:11-12 (THE MESSAGE)

What that means:

Think about other people as much as you do yourself. Serve them whenever you can. You'll find out more about yourself that way than if you're thinking only about yourself.

How to do that:

Think about what you'd like other people to do for you, and do it for them first. Decide how you want to be treated, and treat other people that way. You'll become more You with every kind word you say and every loving thing you do.

"Blessed are the peacemakers, for they will be called sons [and daughters] of God."
— MATTHEW 5:9

What that means:

If you teach people how to cooperate instead of compete, compare, and fight, you are doing what Jesus did (and still does!). The more you become like Jesus, the more you become the real You.

How to do that:

Instead of taking sides in friend fights, help your friends work things out. Instead of watching bullies pick on other kids, stand up for the bullied ones. Instead of listening to gossip, change the subject. It will bring out the best in you, as well as in other people.

When Jesus saw [the invalid] lying there and learned that he had been in this condition for a long time, he asked him, "Do you want to get well?"

"Sir," the invalid replied, "I have no one to help me into the pool when the water is stirred. While I am trying to get in, someone else goes down ahead of me."

Then Jesus said to him, "Get up! Pick up your mat and walk."

– JOHN 5:6-8

What that means:

Instead of stewing over the reasons why things aren't going well, tell them to God. He'll give you what you need to be your whole self. You'll do things you never thought you could!

How to do that:

Say to Jesus, "I want to be all you want me to be. Please show me how." Then get up, ignore the roadblocks you've been allowing to get in your way, and use the things you've learned in this book to walk the journey to your real self. That's the way to be healed and whole. You can do this.

How can a young man [or young woman] keep his
    [or her] way pure?
    By living according to your word.
I seek you with all my heart;
    do not let me stray from your commands.

– PSALM 119:9-10

That Is SO Me!

There are different "travel styles" for this part of your journey. Want to find out what yours is? Read the three solutions to the problem below and decide which one sounds MOST like you. Then read what that might say about you. Remember, each one is a good solution, so there is no right or wrong. There is just You!

Problem:

There's a group of girls in your class who have, for some reason, developed a mean streak. Their latest caper has been spreading a rumor about a new girl who hasn't made any friends yet. It's such an ugly story, nobody will even talk to the new girl. Your true self knows you need to do something.

Solutions:

_____ A. You get all your friends together and announce that something needs to be done about this situation. After all, would any of your group want to be treated that way? You lead your group to the Mean Girls' group and firmly, but politely, inform them that you think what they're doing is wrong. You ask them to stop spreading rumors. Then you and your friends start an all-out campaign to get to know the new girl — inviting her to eat lunch with you, to hang out with you on the playground, and maybe to come to your next sleepover.

_____ B. You go to the girl when she's alone and tell her you're sorry people are saying unkind things about her. The next day you write her a note and ask if she'd like to eat lunch with you and your best friend. You get to know her little by little. One day you see one of the Mean Girls looking at her and whispering to one of her friends. You're nervous but you take a deep breath and go up to the Mean Girl and whisper in *her* ear, asking her to please not spread any more rumors about your friend. Then you smile at her.

_____ C. You go to the new girl on the playground one day, share your granola bar with her, and ask her if the rumor is true. You find out the real story. You go home that night and make a plan. You might get a couple of your friends to help. Over the next few days, you spread the truth about the new girl. Every time somebody says something untrue about her, you tell them they don't know the facts and you correct them. You invite the girl to be in your group when the teacher assigns a project.

What it all means:

If you chose (A), you're all about cool and fun. You like to get out there and just do it — go for it full speed ahead. You are the Energy Champ.

If you chose (B), you're all about being quiet and careful. You slip along on velvet feet, making your way cautiously and softly. You are the Quiet Queen.

If you chose (C), you're all about being thoughtful and intelligent. You think things through, gathering the facts. You measure and analyze and plan. You are the Think Master.

Whatever your true style is, you can SO do what God asks of you — of all of us — to behave as close to the way Jesus did as you possibly can.

Wouldn't it be so cool to make a sound track for your life? You know, a CD of songs that

+ remind you of important times in your life;
+ make you feel a certain way (happy, excited, hopeful);
+ delight you;
+ help you dream; and
+ inspire you to be your best self.

What you'll need:

+ songs that fit the description above (copied from CDs or legally downloaded from the Internet)
+ a blank CD
+ a CD burner

What to do:

+ Listen to lots of music and choose your favorites.
+ Decide what order you want your songs to play in.
+ Rip or download each song, arrange them in a play list, and burn that play list onto a CD.
+ Decide on a name for your sound track and make a label.

What this tells you:

+ what you strive for
+ how you feel things
+ what makes you ask questions
+ what comforts you

What to do now:

⊚ You might listen to your tape when you are
doing your homework;
writing in your journal;
falling asleep;
feeling down;
feeling confused;
trying to make a decision or solve a problem; or
needing to remember who you really are.

⊚ You can add to it whenever you discover a new "life song."

⊚ You can even start a new sound track on every birthday! How cool is that?

That's What I'm Talkin' About!

If I didn't know myself, and I listened to my sound track, I would describe myself as _____

_____

_____

_____

_____

When I made my sound track, _____

_____

_____

_____

_____

_____

_____

(You can write your response in your journal if you want to.)

chapter seven

How You
DOIN'?

Molly couldn't believe it was the last night of camp. Was it really a whole two weeks ago that she'd waved good-bye to her mom and dad with tears streaming down her face?

Now she was sure she would cry tomorrow because she had to leave. But there was no time for that now. She and the other girls in Galilee Cabin still had to come up with a skit for tonight's big event.

"Why do we have to show the most important thing we've learned at camp?" Lydia, of course, whined. "Learning is for school."

"No doubt," Hannah said. "I think our skit should be about the most *fun* thing we did at camp."

"That food fight we had in the dining hall!" somebody said.

"No, it was totally when our cabin won the Water Olympics," somebody else put in.

"I didn't have that much fun," Lydia said with a sniff.

Hannah wiggled her eyebrows. "*I* did."

"*You* had a boyfriend while you were here," Lydia said.

Molly couldn't figure out why that would be fun, but that wasn't the point. "Jerry said the skit had to be about what we learned ... as a cabin," she said.

"Right." Emily bobbed her head up and down. "We definitely learned not to sneak out of the cabin at night."

Hannah and Lydia double-grunted. "Like we can make a whole skit out of that," Lydia said.

"We learned how to clean," Emily said.

"Snore," Hannah said.

There were other suggestions. They learned how to sing "Father Abraham" at warp speed under Emily's coaching; how to kill cockroaches, compliments of Jodi and Paige, two of the rowdies; how to paint their initials on their big toenails, thanks to Hannah; how to whine the alphabet, courtesy of guess who. The only thing they agreed on was that none of those would make a very cool basis for a skit.

And then Molly had an idea. They could do a skit about the one REALLY important thing that at least some of them were starting to learn. The one thing she knew she was never going to forget ...

now what?

Let's leave Molly there while we look one last time at the Unique You adventure. After you've read this chapter, you'll have a chance to write the ending for Molly, in the "That's What I'm Talkin' About!" section. Yours will be the final decision!

That Is SO Me!

The journey to your true self is never over, which is good news. Who would want the Unique You adventure to end?

It's good, though, to stop every now and then to see where you are on the path. Let's do that right now. Remember to be totally honest.

Next to each of the issues below that you've been reading about in this book, write the number of "miles" you think you've "traveled."

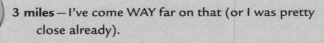

3 miles — I've come WAY far on that (or I was pretty close already).

2 miles — I still have a way to go, but I'm trying.

1 mile — I haven't actually gotten started yet, but I will.

UNIQUE YOU ADVENTURE ISSUES

_____ having attacks of the "Who Am I's"

_____ loving myself

_____ accepting the things I can't change about myself

_____ showing other people who I am

_____ discovering new things about myself

_____ thinking I have to be perfect

_____ trying to keep up with everyone else

_____ trying to fit in

_____ spending some time doing things only I like to do

_____ talking kindly to myself

_____ knowing my limits

_____ comparing myself to other people

_____ loving people the way God wants all of us to

_____ having fun being me

_____ doing what I know is right

Now add up your "miles." You'll come out with a number between 15 and 45. You can write it here: _____

If you have between 45 and 34 "miles," you're on a roll. Keep doing what you're doing and pay careful attention to the areas where you gave yourself less than a 3. Enjoy knowing that you are living a pretty authentic life, and that it's only going to get better!

If you have between 33 and 22 "miles," you have some You work to do, but you're headed in the right direction. Look at the areas where you gave yourself a 1 and try to watch what's happening there. Even the smallest move will eventually get you there, right? Meanwhile, smile, because you're becoming the real You.

If you have 21 to 15 "miles," you're just getting started, but there's nothing wrong with that at all. You have some fun challenges ahead. Just pick one area where you gave yourself a 1 and work on that until you feel pretty comfortable. Then work on another 1. Soon you'll discover that your miles have increased on things you hadn't even worked on. Yeah, baby. You're doin' it!

No matter where you are in the Unique You adventure right now, there are three things to remember as you continue on — things that will make the trip SO much smoother:

#1 — Becoming who you really are takes your whole life. None of us is completely authentic until we're united with God in heaven. It's all about the journey itself. You'll enjoy it more as you grow closer to your true self. Try your best, but never expect to be "done." We often learn the most about ourselves when we aren't sure who we are just then.

#2 — You'll change in many ways as you continue to grow up. The idea is to be as real as you can be at any point on your journey. It'll be so cool to look back from time to time at how far you've come. (That's one of the best reasons for keeping a journal!) And always, deep inside, there will always be the real You that you were born to be.

#3 — You're going to take turns that weren't meant for you. You might even spend weeks, months, even years heading down some "street" that isn't yours. God will lead you back to the right one as long as you stay in touch with him. As soon as he does, put it behind you and move on. You have too much ahead to get stuck in shoulda, woulda, or coulda.

Remember those things, and you'll be all right, girl. You always will be. Because . . .

Peter saw that Jesus really was the Son of God and that he could be — and should be — trusted to teach and lead and save all people. As soon as Peter realized that and believed it, Jesus told Peter who *he* (Peter) was and what he wanted Peter to do.

> "What about you?" [Jesus] asked. "Who do you say I am?"
>
> Simon Peter answered, "You are the Christ, the Son of the living God."
>
> Jesus replied, "Blessed are you, Simon ... for this was not revealed to you by man, but by my Father in heaven. And I tell you that you are Peter, and on this rock I will build my church."
>
> —MATTHEW 16:15-18

It's the same for you. The more you discover that Jesus really is your teacher and your guide and your Savior — and every other truly good thing you can think of — the more clearly he will show you who *you* are and what he wants *you* to do.

So as you continue on with the Unique You adventure, any time you feel lost or confused or just not sure, turn to him and tell him what he means to you. Then all you have to do is pay attention by doing the things we've talked about in this book. Somehow, he'll show You to yourself. Somehow, you will know.

That's What I'm Talkin' About!

Go back to the beginning of this chapter and read about Molly again. Decide what Molly might choose as the subject of their skit. Think about how different Molly is now from the way she was at the beginning of her camp adventure. Imagine what she sees when she looks inside herself now. How will she answer the question "Who am I?"

Now write the story ending, just the way you see it:

_____

_____

_____

_____

_____

_____

_____

_____

_____

_____

_____

EVERYBODY TELLS ME TO BE MYSELF BUT I DON'T KNOW WHO I AM!

You're Good to Go

It's time to give yourself a bon voyage party. You're setting out on an incredible journey, and that calls for a celebration — just for yourself. Here are some celebration ideas, but you are always free to come up with something that is, of course, Uniquely You!

- Give yourself a tea party.
- Take yourself on a backyard picnic.
- Have breakfast in bed.
- Join yourself in an evening of dancing.
- Treat yourself to a music festival with your CD player.
- Invite yourself to an art exhibit of your best work.
- Dribble your basketball (or bat softballs or kick your soccer ball) until you drop.
- Make up a cheer about yourself.
- Build the perfect ice-cream sundae (or pizza or sandwich or giant cookie).
- Toast yourself with a glass of your favorite drink.

One more thing. Be sure to invite God to your celebration. He'll be there. He's been waiting for this all your life.

Read this excerpt from another book in the Faithgirlz! series!

faiThGirLz!

beautyLAB

Nancy Rue

sweet
talk
about
fashion

TAMING
UNTAMABLE
HAIR

FIND YOUR
unique
style

zonderkidz

chapter one

You've Got It
GOIN' ON

The morning Betsy Honeycutt turned eleven, she took a big ol' long look in the mirror, and she didn't like what she saw.

That was pretty weird, since she had seen the very same face the day before (and the day before that and the day before — well, you get the idea), and she hadn't thought much about her freckles or her blue eyes or her honey-brown bob one way or the other. Yesterday she was just Betsy. But today — yikes!

Has my nose always been that long? she thought. *Gross! It looks like a fishhook!*

And what about my eyes? They've gotten closer together — I know they have!

Betsy watched her upper lip curl. Her very thin lip — not plump and luscious like the girls' mouths in the magazines that she'd just fanned across her bed. In fact, there was nothing about her that was even remotely like a model, or, come to think of it, like any of the girls at school that everybody was imitating. She narrowed her eyes at her reflection.

Her hair wasn't long and shiny and thick like Madison's.

Her teeth weren't perfectly white and straight like Taylor's.

And where in the *world* had that *zit* come from? Ashleigh didn't have *zits!*

Betsy gasped right out loud and shoved her face closer to the mirror. It was a pimple between her eyebrows, all right, red and ugly and growing bigger by the millisecond.

She stepped back, hoping it wouldn't look so hideous from farther away, but it was like there was a spotlight shining on it so the entire world could check it out. And not only that, but now she could see her whole self in all her glory.

"Uh, I am *so not* glorious," Betsy said.

The girl in the mirror looked to her like a shapeless blob, dressed in a too-small T-shirt and a too-big pair of shorts that revealed legs hairier than her cocker spaniel's. When she put her hand up to her mouth in disgust, all she saw was the froggy green nail polish she'd put on at last week's sleepover and had been steadily gnawing away at ever since.

"And this is before I turned the lights on," Betsy told the stranger-self. "EWWWWW!"

She turned away from the mirror and looked down at the clear-skinned faces of the perfect girls on the magazine covers. *Will I ever be that pretty?* she thought.

She didn't see how the answer could ever be yes.

now what?

Which of these comes closest to what you were you thinking as you read Betsy's story?

___ I don't get it. I hardly ever hang out looking in the mirror.
___ Um, I kind of like what I see when I look in the mirror.
___ Hello-o! I know exactly how she feels!

Just about every girl between the ages of eight and twelve starts to think—at least a little bit—about the way she looks. But did you know that the minute you're aware that your appearance is a big part of yourself, you're on a journey?

It can be a lifetime of visits to the mirror where you can always find something *wrong*. Or . . . it can be an adventure of discovering the true, absolute, no-denying-it beauty that every girl has—that *you* have.

The choice is pretty much a no-brainer, which is why you have this book in your hand. This book is here to help you set out on the way-fun path to finding your beautiful self. And not just the hair-and-skin-and-clothes outside self, but the unique, one-of-a-kind inside you, which is where real beauty comes from. More on that later.

Before you begin the adventure, it's good to know where you are right now. Write in the space on the next page what you would say to Betsy if you were in her bedroom, watching her suffer in front of the mirror. Look back at what you checked off above to help you. There are no right or wrong answers, so be free and real as you write. If, as you read on in this book, you change your mind about what you want to say to Betsy, you'll have a chance to express that when we get to the end.

Dear Betsy...

When it comes to thinking about the way you look, you're probably somewhere between "What's a mirror?" and "I want to put a bag over my head!" Whatever you think about your beauty, chances are you've gotten some ideas about what beautiful is by looking around and listening. Maybe you've heard things like this:

> "She's so thin. I wish I looked like her."
> "Her skin is perfect. Look at that! I bet she's never had a pimple."
> "Long blonde hair and big blue eyes — now *that's* what I'm talking about."
> "Train to be a model or just look like one! Call now! Operators are standing by!"

To hear people talk, you'd think the only girls who could be considered beautiful are pencil skinny with flawless complexions, long blonde hair, and big blue eyes; and they dress only in the trends that just started this morning. But think about all the girls and women you know that you consider beautiful. Do they all look like that?

What about

❀ your best friend?
❀ your favorite female teacher?
❀ your cool aunt, the cousin you want to be like, and your mom?
❀ And, hey — what about *you*?

Yeah, you. If you counted up all the people who like you and love you, you'd run out of fingers. Ask any one of them if he or she thinks you're a beautiful person, and you'll hear, "Honey, you're drop-dead gorgeous," or something like that.

The point is, no matter what people say about being beautiful, when you get right down to it, the ones who count in your life know real, true, unique beauty when they see it. So how do girls get the idea that they have to look like the cover girl on *Seventeen* to be pretty?

Simple.

From the media. That's TV, movies, billboards, magazines — anything that a lot of people see. The beauties there are all different, but they have one thing in common:

(*Important Thing*):
Don't ask a boy younger than twenty-five. He can't handle questions like that yet. You're sure to get a variation of, "Yeah, if you like baboons," which probably means he likes you — but don't even go there.

they're perfect. Oops — wait. They *look* perfect. But if you met one of them outside the studio, you'd see right away that she has flaws just like everybody else: A piece of hair that won't stay out of her eye; the retainer she just popped in; maybe even a zit — yikes! You don't see those things in an ad or on the movie screen because (1) a team of makeup artists, personal trainers, and wardrobe consultants were all over her before she went before the camera, and (2) film editors can do amazing things with digital enhancing, just the way you can in Photoshop. A couple of clicks and that piece of flyaway hair or that enormous pimple disappears. The eyes are darker. The dress fits better. Get it? A famous model named Cindy Crawford once said, "Even I don't wake up looking like Cindy Crawford."

From models. You may have seen a professional model in person, and she did look pretty perfect to you.

faiThGirLz!

Faithgirlz!–Inner Beauty, Outward Faith

Beauty Lab

ISBN 0-310-71276-9

Beauty tips and the secret of true inner beauty are revealed in this interactive, inspirational, fun addition to the Faithgirlz! line.

Available at your local bookstore!

zonder**kidz**

faiThGirLz!

Faithgirlz!—Inner Beauty, Outward Faith

Sophie Series

Written by Nancy Rue

Sophie LaCroix is a girl like you with adventures in her head, and even bigger ones in her real life! With an imagination that both helps *and* gets her into trouble, Sophie's challenges just keep on coming; but her faith keeps growing too. And so will yours, as you get caught up in the story of this sometimes-dreamy-but-ordinary girl with honest questions about God, friends, family, school, and life—and how to make it all work out.

Visit faithgirlz.com, it's the place for girls ages 8-12
Available at your local bookstore!

zonder**kidz**

faiThGirLz!™

Faithgirlz!–Inner Beauty, Outward Faith

My Faithgirlz! Journal This Girl Rocks!

The questions in this new Faithgirlz! journal focus on your life, family, friends, and future. Because your favorites and issues seem to change every day, the same set of questions are repeated in each section. Includes quizzes to promote reflection and stickers to add fun!

My Faithgirlz! Journal
Spiral, ISBN 0-310-71190-8

NIV Faithgirlz! Backpack Bible

The full NIV text in a handy size for girls on the go—for ages 8 and up.

NIV Faithgirlz! Backpack Bible
Periwinkle Italian Duo-Tone™
ISBN 0-310-71012-X

Available at your local bookstore!

zonder**kidz**

faiThGirLz!

Faithgirlz!–Inner Beauty, Outward Faith

No Boys Allowed
Devotions for Girls
Written by Kristi Holl
This short, 90-day devotional for girls ages 10 and up is written in an upbeat, lively, funny, and tween-friendly way, incorporating the graphic, fast-moving feel of a teen magazine.

Softcover, ISBN 0-310-70718-8

Girlz Rock
Devotions for You
Written by Kristi Holl
In this 90-day devotional, devotions like "Who Am I?" help pave the spiritual walk of life, and the "Girl Talk" feature poses questions that really bring each message home. No matter how bad things get, you can always count on God.

Softcover, ISBN 0-310-70899-0

Chick Chat
More Devotions for Girls
Written by Kristi Holl
This 90-day devotional brings the Bible right into your world and offers lots to learn and think about.

Softcover, ISBN 0-310-71143-6

Shine On, Girl!
Devotions to Keep You Sparkling
Written by Kristi Holl
This 90-day devotional will "totally" help teen girls connect with God, as well as learn his will for their lives.

Softcover, ISBN 0-310-71144-4

Available at your local bookstore!

zonderkidz

faiThGirLz!™

Faithgirlz!—Inner Beauty, Outward Faith

TNIV Faithgirlz! Bible

Hardcover

ISBN 0-310-71002-2

Faux Fur

ISBN 0-310-71004-9

Faithgirlz! is based on 2 Corinthians 4:38: So we fix our eyes not on what is seen, but on what is unseen. For what is seen is temporary, but what is unseen is eternal (NIV)—and helps girls find Inner Beauty, Outward Faith.

You are totally unique and special—and here's a Bible that says that with Faithgirlz! sparkle.

Features include:

- Dream Girl—use your imagination to put yourself in the story
- Bring It On—take quizzes to really get to know yourself
- Is There a Little _____(Eve, Ruth, Isaiah) in You?—see for yourself what you have in common
- Between You and Me—share what you are learning with a friend
- Oh, I Get it!—find answers to Bible questions you've wondered about
- With TNIV text

... And so much more!

Available at your local bookstore!

zonder**kidz**